Flower
of the North

Also by Colleen L. Reece
in Large Print:

Candleshine
Frontiers: Flower of Seattle
Frontiers: Flower of the West
Storm Clouds Over Chantel
To Love and Cherish
A Torch for Trinity
Arizona Angel
Ballad for Nurse Lark
The Calling of Elizabeth Courtland
Friday Flight
A Girl Called Cricket
Mysterious Monday
Legacy of Silver
Saturday Scare

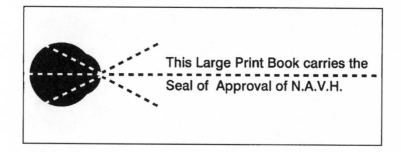

This Large Print Book carries the
Seal of Approval of N.A.V.H.

FRONTIERS:

Flower of the North

Colleen L. Reece

Thorndike Press • Waterville, Maine

Published in 2006 by arrangement with Colleen L. Reece.

Thorndike Press® Large Print Christian Romance.

The tree indicium is a trademark of Thorndike Press.

The text of this Large Print edition is unabridged.
Other aspects of the book may vary from the original edition.

Set in 16 pt. Plantin by Elena Picard.

Printed in the United States on permanent paper.

Library of Congress Cataloging-in-Publication Data

Reece, Colleen L.
    [Flower of the north]
    Frontiers. Flower of the north / by Colleen L. Reece.
       p. cm. — (Thorndike Press large print
Christian romance)
    Originally published as: Flower of the north.
Uhrichsville, OH : Heartsong Presents, 1995.
    ISBN 0-7862-7730-0 (lg. print : hc : alk. paper)
    1. Large type books. I. Title. II. Thorndike Press large
print Christian romance series.
PS3568.E3646F565 2005
813'.54—dc22   2005008506

Flower of the North

As the Founder/CEO of NAVH, the only national health agency solely devoted to those who, although not totally blind, have an eye disease which could lead to serious visual impairment, I am pleased to recognize Thorndike Press* as one of the leading publishers in the large print field.

Founded in 1954 in San Francisco to prepare large print textbooks for partially seeing children, NAVH became the pioneer and standard setting agency in the preparation of large type.

Today, those publishers who meet our standards carry the prestigious "Seal of Approval" indicating high quality large print. We are delighted that Thorndike Press is one of the publishers whose titles meet these standards. We are also pleased to recognize the significant contribution Thorndike Press is making in this important and growing field.

Lorraine H. Marchi, L.H.D.
Founder/CEO
NAVH

* Thorndike Press encompasses the following imprints: Thorndike, Wheeler, Walker and Large Print Press.

Dear Readers,

I hope you enjoy reading the four titles in my American Frontiers Collection as much as I enjoyed writing them.

My deep love for "all things western" began near the small Washington logging town (Darrington) where I was born. I can still picture my two brothers and me gathered around the big woodstove, following the example of our parents, and devouring books by kerosene lamplight.

The more I read, the more I dreamed of growing up and someday writing a book. My desire to write deepened when our family camped throughout the western United States, thrilling to the mountains and canyons, rivers and deserts Zane Grey and others described so well. Little did I know those trips were laying a foundation for my "someday." Or that "someday" I would author more than 140 books with total sales over three million copies.

I thank God for my "frontier-like" background and for being able to offer readers *"Books You Can Trust"* (my motto) that help make the world a little better place. Providing inspiration, joy, and encouragement is my way of saying thanks to the wonderful authors who did the same for a shy, small town girl whose parents long ago taught to dream big.

Chapter 1

The setting sun fired a parting ray before it dropped behind the Philadelphia skyline. The beam sped to the depths of a great white diamond in a golden circle and turned the stone in the ring redder than spilled blood.

Atop a hill that afforded a spectacular view of the city, Bernard Clifton shuddered, then called himself a fool. "Too many surgeries in a row," he muttered. Tall, dark, and commanding, his soot-black eyes watched the fire in the diamond and heavens turn cold. After the last gleam died, he closed the white velvet box in his tanned hand and pocketed it. A few hours from now, the tiny ring would rest on Julia Langley's slim, white finger — a setting fitting even for the rare diamond's glory. Once there, the world would know he had won, again. The world and Arthur Baldwin, Bern's arch rival.

Regret clouded the lean, high-cheek-boned face that attracted interest in spite of its cragginess and lack of beauty. He and Arthur had changed from friendly rivals to bitter enemies, doggedly fighting for position, adhering to the creed "You get what you take and no more." Yet all through college and medical school they had been brothers. Others called them the David and Jonathan of the prestigious eastern institutions where they excelled and good-naturedly shared honors in athletics and courses without malice. Competition had brought out the best in each. Then.

Now on this spring evening in 1893, Bern shook his head and started home. For the past year, almost to the day, he and Arthur had forsaken any attempt at civility. Clashes over ball games and field events, the fierce desire for first place class standing had continued. Yet both knew their conflict had little to do with such trivial things.

Long strides of Bern's powerfully muscled legs took him down from the heights to the city below. Lighted windows offered refuge against the growing dark, protection from the night. Fearless as he was, those pale yellow squares spelled welcome to the man with a future in his pocket far brighter than the ring hidden there.

Behind one of the windows Dad waited, just as he'd always done: first for the small, motherless boy who often scorned companions to come home to a sickly father; then, for a stripling lad whose exploits and great physical strength brought popularity and a full scholarship to one of the great universities. Now, he awaited the son succeeding in rigid medical school studies.

"Can we afford it, Dad?" How many times had Bern asked the question. "With you not able to work much, shouldn't I stop school and earn a living?"

"We'll get by." The pale-faced father with shadowed eyes inevitably smiled. "Remember, I inherited a tidy sum from my parents. We will never be rich, that is, until you're a leading surgeon, but we have enough."

Once he added, "You must never give up your medical profession, Bernard. God has given you a great talent to heal. Promise me that no matter what happens, you won't let your talent dwindle and die."

The intensity in his father's face elicited a quick, careless promise from Bernard. "Sure, Dad. But what do you think is going to happen? You aren't feeling worse, are you?"

"On the contrary. I walked a half-mile today and will walk more tomorrow. First thing you know, I'll be racing alongside you on your college field!"

Bern's growing expertise in diagnosis didn't see that happening, but Dad certainly looked better than he had in years. Perhaps the joy of his son's achievements helped him. Some of the professors strongly believed physical health and being content walked together. Dad had a different explanation, a verse from the Bible: Proverbs 17:22. He often quoted, "A merry heart doeth good like a medicine: but a broken spirit drieth the bones."

Bern only half-listened. He believed in God but didn't have time to read the Bible. His college and medical books required his full attention if he were to excel. Once he jokingly demanded, "What are you, a preacher?" His father muttered something inaudible and left the room.

Bern's straight black brows met over his keen eyes. Strange thing for Dad to do. He never resented his son's joking. A few minutes later his father returned, his face calm as usual.

"Are you prepared for your pharmacology exam?" he asked. The following conversation effectively drove away any further wonder, and day after busy day rushed past to bury personal problems or thoughts under a welter of school activities, medical practice, and the like.

His blood racing, a quick sprint ended Bern's descent and brought him to the modest but comfortable cottage he and his father shared. He flung open the door and sniffed. Good. Beef stew. After tossing his hat and coat in the direction of the hall closet, Bern wandered into the kitchen.

"Mmm. Smells good. Fresh bread, too." He inhaled deeply. "Dad, you're a wonder."

"Because I can cook?" The prematurely white-haired man turned an amused gaze at his son.

"No." He sprawled in a chair at the simply laid table. "You just are."

"I hope you'll always think so."

A certain note in the older man's voice cut through Bern's reverie. "No reason I shouldn't." One fine hand, with its strong, tapering fingers envied by companions who longed for his skill in surgery, crept to the little white box. The desire to show Dad the ring overwhelmed him, but he hesitated. How much better simply to present Julia as his fiancée. *A lot better,* he told himself. Dad had met her at a college tea, but Bern hadn't confessed he'd fallen madly in love with Julia the first night he saw her. *If she chose Arthur . . .*

The thought set his heart thumping harder than it had ever done before, even during the hard-fought, harder-won races and football games. Blood pounded in his ears the same way it did when he raced nimbly down the field in a zigzag course and eventually reached the goal under seemingly impossible odds. The memories brought a smile. The dark eyes that never failed to soften at the sight of anything hurt or wounded yet could turn rock-hard with determination reflected tiny yellow flames from the lamp on the table. *Soon,* he told himself. *If Julia says yes . . .* A flutter of unease similar to what he'd experienced on the hilltop blew across his heart. Surely she would accept him and not just for the ring he carried.

Peace returned and he attacked the dinner with a raging appetite.

"We don't get this kind of food at the hospital," he said through a mouthful of expertly seasoned stew.

"So that's why you come home, to get fed."

Bern grinned. "One of the reasons."

He finished his dinner, accepted seconds, and gulped down the food. "Sorry, Dad. I don't have much time." He sighed. "Know something? One of the things I'll be glad for once I'm practicing is not having to gulp my food all the time. I can count on the fingers of one hand and have some left over the meals I haven't had to rush in the last month." He stood and started for the door.

"Bernard, have you and Arthur had a falling out? You never mention him."

The quiet voice caught Bern midstride to the hall for his coat. He longed to tell his father the whole story and receive justification. *No,* he thought, *not until the gleaming golden ring adorns Julia's soft hand.* "Sorry, Dad. I have to rush. Good night."

"Good night." The sound rang like a benediction along with the closing of the front door. Bern stepped into the night. Some unexplainable feeling made him turn on his heel. He could see his father at the kitchen table. Even while he watched, Dad's head bowed. His shoulders shook.

Bern took a quick step back, his gaze fixed on the window. *Dad must be sick.* He took a second step and stopped, transfixed by the agonized look in the white face. Not illness but naked pain showed, even in the

15

soft lamplight. A feeling of helplessness went through Bern. Even a beloved son could not intrude on such a moment. He turned away and decided to walk the two miles to the Langley home. It would provide time for him to think.

What is it? The picture of his father at the table had dimmed some of the radiance of the coming interview. Curious tricks of light and shadow often distorted features, he comforted himself. Again his fingers stole to his pocket. Before long he'd see Julia, small, blond, and beautiful. The spring night around him faded, replaced by an equally lovely spring night just a year earlier.

"Come on, Bern. You can't study all the time." Arthur Baldwin's happy-go-lucky countenance hid a brilliant mind behind his cherublike face. As fair as Bernard was dark, Arthur slapped his friend's shoulder while Bern hunched over his desk studying. "How long has it been since you went to any of the college functions?"

"Don't have time," Bern retorted. "Neither do you, if you want to beat me out in tomorrow's exam."

"Then let's call it a draw and take the evening off," Arthur coaxed. He pompously drew himself up. "Besides, you know as well as I if you get the name of being a grind, you won't get ahead. Man, this reception is important! Any time a professor gives something for medical students, he expects them to be there. Climb into your dress suit and let's go."

Bernard tilted back his straight chair, hard enough to keep even a weary student awake, until it creaked. "You really think I should go?" He doubtfully eyed the piles of paper, the open texts. "There's just so much to learn."

"The reception only lasts a couple of hours." Arthur threw open the armoire and extracted Bern's clothes. "Climb into these, will you?"

A half-hour later, immaculate and correctly garbed, Bern followed Arthur into the ballroom of the host professor's mansion. With the ease of long practice, he smiled politely and murmured pleasantries while half his brain wrestled with the problem he'd been doing when Arthur kidnapped him. Bern little noted what he ate or who said what to him until — "Miss Langley, may I introduce my friend, Mr. Clifton?"

Bern absently turned toward Arthur, his mind still considering and rejecting the

17

worth of certain procedures. "It's a pleasure to meet you." He reached to take the young lady's lace-mittened hand, then glanced at her face, barely stifling a gasp. An exquisite face peered up at him from under an azure chiffon hat that matched precisely her fluffy gown. Eyes of a little deeper blue sparkled. Yellow curls soft and fine as a child's haloed the white face and pink cheeks. She reminded him of apple blossoms and roses, sunshine and cloudless skies. He couldn't help staring.

Small pearly teeth sparkled in a lovely smile. "I believe I've seen you on the playing field, Mr. Clifton." Miss Langley freed her hand and clasped both together. "Indeed, aren't you the one who made the winning score at the last football game in your senior year of college?"

Bern actually found himself blushing. "Arthur has evidently been talking." He gave his grinning friend a furious glance.

"I found it quite interesting." She smiled again, closing them into a small complete circle that excluded others and promised all kinds of delightful times in their future acquaintance. "Dear me, I've promised Mama to help make the students feel at home. Mr. Baldwin, Mr. Clifton, do come to call soon." She drifted away with a flirtatious sweep of the ridiculously long lashes that rested on her cheeks in little half-moons.

"Well, what do you think of her?" Arthur asked the minute she moved out of hearing.

"Who *is* she?"

"Didn't you hear me introduce her? She's Professor Langley's daughter." His eyes sparkled with fun. "She's just home from several years studying abroad at fashionable schools."

"Is she married or engaged?"

Some of the laughter faded. "I wish she were. To me."

Bern yanked his gaze from the graceful girl and turned toward his friend. "Are you in love with her? Has she given you reason to think she might — care?" His hands clenched. He dreaded the answer but must know.

"Every man who meets her falls in love with her," Arthur carelessly said. "As for her caring, who knows?" He shrugged.

"Then if I were to win her, it wouldn't be an unfair thing."

"Win her! Are you mad? Julia Langley won't give up her queen position for any man." Dull red suffused Arthur's fair skin. "She sits in her ivory tower with all her vassals at her feet." His fine mouth set in a hard line.

"How can you speak so of that innocent girl?" Bern kept his voice low, but fury ran through his every word. "You should be horsewhipped."

A dangerous gleam crept to Arthur's eyes. "And you think you're the one to do it? Look, Bern, everything that's beautiful on the outside isn't necessarily the same on the inside. I'm telling you, she's trouble. According to gossip, she leads men to the point of distraction, then turns down their proposals."

"In my presence you will hereafter refer to her as Miss Langley, not Julia." His eyelids half closed, he looked at Arthur coldly. "I don't believe she's capable of what you say, but if it's true, why do you want to marry her?"

"She might settle down and make a good wife to the right man." Arthur sounded dubious, but he met Bern's gaze squarely.

"You?"

Arthur shrugged again. "Perhaps. Perhaps not." He smiled his most insouciant grin. "I'm going to try for her and take my chances."

"So am I."

"You aren't serious!" Arthur's grin

faded. His blue eyes flashed. "Only bounders cut in on their friends."

"You just said she's given you no particular attention," Bern reminded. "Why shouldn't I see if I can win Miss Langley's affections?" He laughed mockingly. "Haven't we always competed? Why be different now?" He held out his strong hand. "Let the best man win, Arthur."

Baldwin hesitated perceptibly before a confident smile restored his charm. "Thanks, I will." He gripped the extended hand. His blond hair tossed like a mane. "I'm giving you fair warning. I intend to marry Ju— Miss Langley."

"So do I." Bern had never been surer of anything in his life. She had burst upon him like the beams from a skyrocket. He felt invincible, able to do anything. Arthur might be a worthy opponent, but he'd bested his friend before; he would do it again and walk off with Julia, the crowning achievement. With a wife like that, nothing on earth could stop him from becoming the top surgeon in Philadelphia, nay, New York itself. Once established here, why stop? He would lay the world at her daintily slippered feet.

Emboldened by his dreams, Bernard Clifton laid them before the object of his

intense adoration the first time he called.
"Miss Langley, I feel it only fair to tell you
I intend to marry you and make you queen
of Philadelphia, then New York."

Her eyes glistened even though a barb
marred her laugh. "Indeed, Mr. Clifton.
What makes you think I want such a
place?"

"Don't you?" Never one to quibble, he
stared straight into her blue eyes.

She carelessly laughed and rose to cross
the small morning room where she had received him. *What a picture she made
when she seated herself on a bench in
front of a highly polished spinet and tinkled merry tunes with her white fingers!*
Bern admiringly thought.

Arthur found them so, the pink-clad girl
a vision of beauty, the dark Bern sitting
cross-armed. A frown of annoyance
crossed his face, but he quickly hid it and
exerted himself to win the attention Julia
distributed impartially between them.

The stage was set for this strange three-
cornered relationship in coming weeks and
months. One week Julia drifted toward one
more, the next, the other. Gradually she
dismissed other callers in favor of the ex-
citing contest between the two strong men.
When Professor Langley took his daughter

to task and sternly admonished her, she only smiled. "Can I help it if neither of them will give in?" she innocently asked.

"Why don't you choose one and let the other go?" he demanded. "You are tearing down a friendship that's been the talk of campus and hospital, Julia."

"Why, Papa!" She produced a convincing tear. "As if I'd do such a thing." She dabbed at her eyes with a scrap of handkerchief. "As for choosing, how can I?" Her small hands fluttered like white butterflies. "They're both so splendid. Tell me, if you were a girl, who would you choose?"

The professor considered. "Either of them is too good for you, miss. You'd do better to take Baldwin. He's not so idealistic and won't require perfection. I'm not sure you can live up to Clifton. I believe he would be rather terrible concerning his possessions."

"Possessions! As if I'll ever just be that," Julia sniffed at the idea.

"On the other hand," Professor Langley continued. "In spite of Baldwin's brilliance, I believe Clifton will go farther. There's something about him, a certain ruthlessness, that's going to put him on top and keep him there. If you want to rule society and are willing to give in a bit, take Clifton."

"I'll never give in to any man," she announced. "Besides, Bernard idolizes me. He will do anything to please me."

"I wouldn't count on it," her father retorted. "No minister's wife will ever have to walk the straight and narrow any more than you will, should you become Mrs. Bernard Clifton!"

Julia merely smiled, and after their talk, became more available to Bern and less to Arthur. She listened to her suitor's grandiose plans for the future and smiled again. Still, in a private interview she sighed and told Arthur, "I *am* fond of you. If it weren't for Bernard, I might even care enough to marry you."

Fathoms in love with the fickle girl, Arthur caught her hand. "Julia, don't tease. Do you really mean that?"

"Of course I do." Her blue eyes opened wide. "How can you doubt me?"

At that moment, memories of the priceless friendship Arthur and Bern once shared faded. Anger rose in Arthur. *Hadn't he warned his friend only bounders cut in?* According to Julia herself, she cared, or would if Bern hadn't butted in where he knew he wasn't wanted. A series of minor defeats at the other's hands added salt to Arthur's fresh wound: Bern, given charge of a special patient; Bern, with a slight scholastic edge. Bern, Bern, Bern! From the spirit of challenge, Arthur found himself brooding over old defeats. He jealously hoarded every moment he could spend with Julia, to the detriment of his work. The academic gap between Bern and him widened. Arthur couldn't concentrate, torn between love and resentment. It made him even more furious. A few feeble attempts by Bern to reestablish their old comradeship earned rebuffs, although deep inside Arthur missed it more than he cared to own.

So, on the anniversary of the event that led to the corrosion of an iron-strong fellowship, Bernard Clifton walked alone through the streets of Philadelphia, not at all certain Julia would accept his ring, or him. His surprisingly sensitive lips grew grim. She'd give him an answer tonight or not at all. Twelve tedious months spent waiting had succeeded in separating him from Arthur, though the memories were still vivid. *Why hadn't Julia realized what her dallying about making a decision would do?* Bern agonized. If she'd chosen

Arthur, Bern would have accepted it. Despite their estrangement, he also believed Arthur would have done the same. The first few months of courtship had been exhilarating. He'd seen Arthur change, though, from lighthearted to miserable. If Bern himself didn't love Julia to distraction, he'd have stepped aside long ago.

Once Bern mentioned to her the havoc her indecision had created. The resulting flood of tears left him feeling he'd been a brute. Surely no one so innocent would deliberately set out to destroy! Yet, try as he might, Bern couldn't quite forget Arthur's words at that first reception. *She leads men to the point of distraction, then turns down their proposals.* Why couldn't he squash the warning, as Arthur himself appeared to have done? He squared his shoulders and for the first time in weeks found himself praying. "Please, she's so sweet. Make everything be all right." He felt no better. *Should he have told God outright how much he wanted Julia?* Bern snorted. A God worth believing in already knew.

He looked up to the stars, serene, shining steadily on a troubled world and an even more troubled man. Wispy clouds covered part of the moon and gave it a leering look. The fancy made him wonder. How could he expect anything from a God he ignored most of the time? A longing swept through him. On impulse he cried into the night, "It won't always be like this. As soon as I finish my studies and get established, I'll have more time. For You, I mean."

Only the distant barking of a dog answered. Bern realized he stood before the red brick Langley mansion. He slowly opened the gate, walked the length of the well-manicured drive, and lifted the door knocker.

"Evenin', Dr. Clifton." A beaming butler opened the door.

"Not Doctor yet." Bern laughed and surrendered his coat and hat to the friendly servant. "Soon though, Thomas. Miss Julia is expecting me, I believe."

"Yes, sir. Right this way."

I never want a butler, Bern told himself on the way down the long hall with its stuffy looking portraits and velveteen draperies, hoping the straight-backed Thomas didn't read his thoughts. *I suppose Julia will, though. It's what she is used to.* He realized they had never talked about such things. He frowned. They usually talked about Julia or how much he loved her and what he'd provide for her. The idea struck him unpleasantly and he pushed it aside as disloyal. Once she accepted his ring, things would change.

The elegant room to which Thomas led him offered a perfect setting for the demurely seated girl who greeted him with a smile. She wore something white and fluffy and her yellow curls gleamed in the light of many candles. "I thought it cozier than a harsher light," she said.

Bern seated himself next to her. Now that the moment he'd dreamed of had actually arrived, he found himself breathless. Before he could do more than take her hands, Julia eagerly asked, "Isn't it splendid?" Her laugh tinkled like the music from her spinet. "Father said I mustn't let on I know, but after all, who has a better right?" She actually squeezed his hands in her excitement.

"Know what?"

"Didn't you get a certain letter today?" she demanded. "One offering you the fine position in Philadelphia's best hospital? The same position every student in your class has been hoping for?"

"Why, yes, but how did you know?" Bern blinked.

"I arranged it, of course." She prattled

on, but he missed most of what she said.

"You mean Professor Langley recommended me?" His heart leaped at the thought.

"Father? Of course not. I talked with the hospital director. He's an old friend and wants me to be happy." She laughed triumphantly, and a look he couldn't understand crept into her small face.

A fine white line encircled Bern's mouth. His eyes darkened and he pulled free. "You mean I am being hired because of your influence and not my qualifications?"

"What difference does it make, darling? You're graduating summa cum laude. Don't be so serious. I wanted to make you happy." A ready tear fell.

He automatically comforted her, telling himself she couldn't realize that in her desire to please, she'd overstepped the bounds. Yet the prize plum he'd coveted tasted bitter from knowing someone else had plucked and handed it to him.

Chapter 2

Bern suppressed an involuntary pang of disappointment. He hadn't even told Dad he'd won the illustrious position. Anticipation of his father's surprise and delight when the announcement was made at graduation had silenced him. Julia must never know the bitterness of soul her thoughtless act had brought. He reached for the ring that symbolized his love. Fancy speeches fled. He tilted her soft chin up until he could look into her eyes. Something flickered in their blue depths, but he could not identify it. "Julia," he abruptly said. "Will you marry me?"

Her expression changed to the enchantment that first lured him. "Of course, darling. Why do you think I arranged for your appointment to the hospital?"

Something in him rebelled and the question came, *Would she have married you if there had been no fine job, no fame and fortune?* He sternly resisted the longing to ask her. It should be enough that she'd chosen him. Yet for the second time disappointment beat against him like ocean waves on a rocky shore. He stifled a sigh and tried to recapture the high moment he had anticipated. In a quick motion, he brought forth the white velvet case and silently handed it to her.

Julia's fingers greedily snapped the spring. The case opened and the diamond shone brilliantly. "Oooh," she crooned and slid it on her finger. "It's so big!" He winced at the avid note in her voice and the way she preened, moving her hand to and fro before she said, "It's larger than any of my friends' stones." In a rare gesture of affection, she flung herself into his arms. For the first time his lips touched hers. Until then, she had properly turned her face to one side so he merely grazed a rounded cheek. Her cool kiss set his pulses pounding. His arms went around her, and he would have kissed her again, but she drew away, flushed and laughing.

"We must show Papa and Mama my ring." She gracefully stood and he rose with her.

"Julia?" A wistful tone crept into his voice. "Do you love me?"

"Of course I do, silly." She patted his cheek with a pink palm, then lightly ran from the room and down the long hall. "Mama, Papa, just see what Bern gave me."

He slowly followed. Arthur's belief that Julia would settle down once married offered little comfort. She had sounded so matter of fact when she confirmed that she loved him. He'd heard her say she loved a new hat in the same manner. His hands clenched and he vowed to make her love him the way he did her. One day she'd come to him freely and then . . .

"Bernard, are you never coming?" Her petulant voice shattered his reverie, and he strode down the hall and into the fire-warmed library to greet the older Langleys. Suddenly aware of Mrs. Langley's hesitancy, he realized he'd committed a social blunder. Although they knew he'd paid court, Bern had never asked for official permission to marry their daughter.

He blurted out, "I should have asked before I gave her the ring. I apologize. May I marry your daughter?"

"Of course." Professor Langley held out a welcoming hand. "If you think you can handle her and make her happy."

"I can."

His quick reply brought a smile to the couple's faces and a small frown to Julia's, but the sparkling ring effectively silenced her.

"When shall we tell your father?" She turned her hand to catch the full effect of the diamond's glory in the dancing flames from the fireplace. Again it shone red. Again, for no apparent reason, Bern shivered.

"Is he aware you planned to ask Julia to marry you?" the professor asked.

"No. I wanted to wait until . . ."

"I understand." A look in his kind eyes showed how well the professor knew his only child. "Perhaps you would like to tell him when you return home tonight. We can arrange a meeting between the families to discuss details later, if you like."

Relief surged through him and he wished he'd given Dad a hint earlier. Bern remembered the bent head and shaking shoulders. "He didn't seem well tonight, sir. If you and Mrs. Langley will excuse me, I'll just tell Julia good night and go. I want to check on him."

"Well, I like that." His fiancée's pink lips pouted. "We're only just engaged and you're hurrying away?"

"I'm afraid you'll have to get used to it if

you're going to be a doctor's wife," he teased, although secretly pleased at the apparent sign she cared.

"Perhaps." An inscrutable look crossed her face, but she tucked one hand under his arm and paced the long hall to the door with him. "I'll see you tomorrow?"

"Of course." He held her close and looked above her head at the portraits of long-dead ancestors, neither seeing nor caring about them. His earlier depression had vanished. How could any man who held the world in his arms be happier?

The two miles between the Langley mansion and the Clifton home vanished beneath Bern's fast pace. Even though more mist completely covered the moon, enough stars plus the lighted windows cleared the way for him. He lost himself in rosy dreams. Would Julia consent to a wedding shortly after graduation? The hospital position meant money enough to provide a nice home. Later they could build whatever she wanted.

By the time he reached home, Bern had decided to tell his father about his honor. It didn't seem fair for Julia and her parents to know. Neither could he trust her to keep the secret in the few weeks remaining before graduation. He grinned, barely able to wait. He'd casually mention the position, then add the news of his marriage. Dad would be thrilled with both.

For the second time that day, Bern bounded into the house. He left his hat and coat in the hall and stepped into the cozy room he preferred to the more formal parlor. His father sat in a comfortable chair, his Bible in his lap. Bern wondered a little. Dad seemed to have discarded most of his other reading material in favor of the Bible, at least on the evenings his son was there. Bern threw himself on a sofa the other side of a heavy, magazine-piled table and stretched out.

"I have something to tell you."

A curious stillness surrounded his father, almost as though he was bracing himself.

"The letter that came today. I've been offered the job at the biggest hospital here in Philadelphia, the one I told you about." He couldn't keep the elation from his announcement.

His father visibly relaxed. "That's wonderful!" The older man's face shone. He rose from his chair, hands held out toward Bern.

"There's more. I asked Julia Langley to marry me. Dad, she accepted! I didn't know if she would. Arthur's been after her for months. That's the reason — Dad, what's wrong?" Bern sprang from the sofa and stared at the ashen-faced man who tottered toward him, hands still extended but shaking.

"No, no, no!" A cry like that of a wounded animal burst from the older man's throat. His eyes glazed and he took an unsteady step forward. Unseeing, unheeding, his foot hit the table leg and he lost his balance. His body twisted in an effort to break the fall. Before Bern could catch him, his father's head struck the corner of the table with a sickening thud. He hit the floor, an unconscious, crumpled heap.

"Dad!" Rigid medical training released Bern from his stupor. He fell to his knees. Crimson blood spurted from a gash in his father's pale forehead. Bern used the heel of his hand to stanch the flow and let out a bellow he hoped some neighbor would hear. When no one responded, he shouted again at the top of lungs made mighty by hard exercise and running. "Help, someone!"

Running steps and a loud pounding at the door rewarded his efforts. "Clifton? You all right?" The door flew open. A burly neighbor and his son raced through the hall and into the parlor. "What happened?"

"He fell. Bring a carriage. We have to get him to the hospital."

Bern felt he'd wandered into a nightmare that didn't end. He held his father's limp body in strong arms while the neighbor drove the carriage in a wild rush through the night to the closest hospital. He refused to leave during the examination in spite of the attending physician's request.

"I'm in my last weeks of medical training. He's my father. I won't leave him."

The doctor eyed the keen stare and steady but pale face. "All right, then. But keep back. He's our patient, not yours."

Respect for his elders brought a reluctant, "Yes, sir," but he watched every part of the examination with sharp hawklike eyes that missed nothing. Once the doctor grunted. He finished his task and ordered, "Get him cleaned up and put him in a private room. He needs someone on duty —"

"That won't be necessary. I'll stay," Bern interrupted.

The doctor nodded briefly. "I don't find any evidence of a skull fracture. There doesn't appear to be pressure on the brain. However, the blow may have caused a stroke. We won't know until he regains consciousness. All we can do is wait."

Wait. The most horrible word in the world. *Well, at least I'll be with Dad,* Bern told himself. Sudden compassion for all who waited in hopes of healing for their loved ones filled him. In the eternity following, his dark gaze never left the still figure whose spotless bandages were a little whiter than the patient's face. If only he were finished with his studies! If only he knew more.

When his father's condition remained the same in the morning, Bern left just long enough to arrange for a few days leave of absence from his studies and hospital work. He came back armed with enough textbooks to fill a well. Hour after hour he read everything he could find on head wounds and their possible complications. His eyes burned. He forgot Arthur and their feud, Julia, honors and fame, everything but the need to help his father.

For the next three days Bern haunted the hospital. The attending physician came each night and morning, examined his patient, and shook his head.

"No change." He ordered a cot brought in and trays of food. When Bern objected, he barked, "You either eat and sleep or out you go." On the fourth morning he looked into the haggard face and said, "You can't afford to keep missing classes and ward work. There's nothing you can do here."

Fire flashed from Bern's dark eyes. "You think I'd leave him?"

The doctor exploded. "Think it over, Clifton. What's it going to do to him when he wakes up to find you've flunked your final year of training on his account? Man, it could set him back. I wouldn't want to take that chance. Do you?"

Never give up your medical profession, Bernard. Promise.

Sure, Dad.

Bern's body jerked. He stared at the physician. "All right. It's what Dad would want." He strode out, head high to keep back tears of pain and weariness.

With the discipline gained from long practice, he forced himself to write the papers, take the exams, and attend the patients assigned to him. When his father's pale face intruded between him and whatever he had to do, Bern gritted his teeth and doggedly stuck to his job. New lines that had not been in his face a week before appeared. He said little to anyone and after an explanatory note to Julia, put aside his desire to be with her. Time enough for that later.

A few days later his father opened his eyes. Bern sprang from the chair beside him. "You fell and hit your head." He smiled. "You're going to be all right."

A strangled sound came from the patient.

"Don't try to talk," his son warned.

His eyes closed again, but this time the even breathing showed the elder Clifton had fallen into a natural sleep. He awakened again during the doctor's visit that evening. This time he tried to say something, but no words came out. Terror filled his eyes and his clutching hands picked at the sheet.

During the examination, Bern bit the inside of his mouth until he could taste blood. When it ended, he gave a sigh of relief. Other than not being able to formulate words, his father appeared little damaged. The wound on his head had begun to heal. He could move his legs, arms, fingers, and toes on command.

"Don't worry about the speech," the gruff physician told his patient. "Quite often this happens. Rest and give your body time to heal."

Yet when after several more days Clifton still couldn't speak, the doctor beetled his brows and took Bern aside. "Is there anything else I need to know? Your father acts like a man in shock. What was he doing just before he fell? Is he under some kind of mental strain?" He listened to Bern's halting explanation in silence, especially the part when his patient had leaped up and shouted protests against his son's engagement.

"Does he dislike Miss Langley? Can he be jealous, afraid of losing you? It could explain a lot."

"He only met her once and commented later how attractive she was. Dad isn't the jealous kind. In fact, as far back as I can remember, he always encouraged me to have other friends." Memory of Arthur and their happy times came to mind. If only they could go back! Of course, they couldn't. Arthur would never forgive his friend for what he considered as intruding.

Except for his lack of speech, Clifton improved rapidly. Before long Bern could take him home. He arranged with the helpful neighbor's wife to come in and clean and cook, and he hired their son to stay nights when he himself couldn't be there.

A week later, Arthur appeared at Bern's open door. He hesitated on the threshold, then stepped inside and closed it behind him.

"Sorry about your father." He cleared his husky throat. "Uh, I kept informed."

Bern warmed to him. Could Dad's accident be the key to unlocking the hostility between them? "Thanks. I'll tell him you asked about him. He always thought a great deal of you."

"Too bad his son changed." The glitter in Arthur's blue eyes acted like a cold glass of water thrown in Bern's tired face. "Once before I warned you. Now I'm doing it again." He stared at the seated man, hatred written all over him. "What a fool I was to believe you'd fight fair."

"Just what have I done that isn't?" A razor edge came into Bern's voice. He shoved back his chair, knowing and dreading the answer before it came.

"As if you don't know," his visitor sneered. "I wouldn't have believed you'd use a woman's wiles to beat me out." Contempt oozed from him. "That's too low even for me."

Bern felt the blood drain from his face. Yet some new maturity gained through the long, frightening nights watching his father tempered the desire to pound Arthur Baldwin into a pulp. "I didn't send her. I didn't even know she knew or planned to approach the hospital director."

"That's not what Julia says."

"Liar!" Bern took a step toward him.

"Oh? I left her admiring the rock of a diamond you gave her and gloating." His voice changed to a shrill but unmistakable falsetto. " 'Oh, Arthur, surely you understand how it is.' I understand, all right. You're a sneak and a coward and have earned the right to be treated as such. Watch out, Bernard Clifton. The mightiest trees fall with the loudest crashes." His voice broke in what sounded like a sob and he slammed the door open, went out, and banged it behind him.

Bern fell back into his chair. A wave of nausea rose. Had Julia really taunted Arthur? Yet long after he turned out his study light and tossed sleeplessly, he remembered most of all the terrible disillusionment in his former friend's face.

Arthur Baldwin's breath came in great, ragged gasps as he rushed down the rough street and away from Bernard's room. Deep in Arthur's heart he hadn't believed Bern would stab him in the back, yet the evidence lay before him. Bern got the job, Bern got the girl. Anger blacker than the clouds that boiled up across the city sank into the bested man's heart. He clenched his fist and shook it at the sky. "I'll get him. I'll see him in the dust." His excited fancy seized on what Julia had told him. "If it weren't for him, she'd marry me." His keen mind worried the idea like a cat with a mouse. How could he put Bern in a bad light before the Langleys?

"They pride themselves on honor and right living," he muttered. "At least, the professor and his wife do. Julia just wants attention." A large raindrop splashed on his hand. Then another. With them came the gem of an idea. What if he could prove his antagonist unworthy of their daughter? He sighed. No hint of scandal had ever touched the Cliftons, except. . . . What did anyone know of the mother? Who was she? Where did she come from? An undesirable background would be more than enough to break up the engagement. All Arthur knew of Mrs. Clifton was what Bern had told him: She'd died when he was born.

An ugly smile spoiled Arthur's sunny face even as ugly thoughts took root in his mind. "I'll do it," he vowed.

Never one to hesitate, the very next day Arthur Baldwin approached the most highly rated and successful detective agency in Philadelphia. He pulled a great wad of money from his pocket and threw it on the desk in front of a sharp-eyed man who merely raised his brows. He'd seen such sums before and shied away from them. "We don't kill people," he tersely responded.

Arthur gulped; his face paled. "I don't want anyone killed," he protested.

"Then what do you want and why are you willing to pay so highly?"

"A man has cheated me out of everything I want in life," Arthur blurted out. "I want you to investigate his dead mother, grandparents, anyone in his family who might throw a stain on him." He clamped his lips in a grim line.

"And just who might this man be? I'll need names, dates, places."

Arthur gave them, his face flushed. "How long will it take? There's plenty more money if this isn't enough."

"You sure must hate the guy," the investigator observed as he lighted a pipe. Soon, blue smoke half-hid his face.

Arthur left without answering, and the observant man he'd just hired smiled cynically. He'd know before nightfall who the client calling himself Dan Brown really was and why he had it in for a certain Bernard Clifton. He stretched and yawned. It was his business to know. He picked up the money and smiled again. Pretty little hunk of cash for what looked like a routine job. A few telegrams to fellow investigators scattered around the country should do it.

Filled with excitement over what he had just done, Arthur literally returned to the scene of the crime — the Langley mansion. He secretly rejoiced to find Julia alone and sulky over what she viewed as Bern's neglect. In consequence, she treated Arthur as confidant and poured out all her imagined troubles. She ended by plaintively saying, "I'm not sure I'd have taken the ring, gorgeous as it is, if I'd known Bernard intended to play nursemaid to a father who can be better taken care of by servants."

Arthur rashly spoke out of his guilty conscience. "Suppose you found out he wasn't what you thought, that there were things in his life . . ." He let his voice die mysteriously, wondering if even an investigator could unearth anything the Langleys would condemn. "What if someone else offered you an even bigger ring? What then, Julia?"

"What do you mean? Do you have someone in mind, in case that happened?"

"I might." He smiled the open smile that robbed his face of any duplicity.

"I don't know." She glanced down, then

up through her long lashes. "Papa and Mama are only waiting until after graduation to announce the engagement. Papa said Bernard had enough on his mind just finishing his exams and caring for his father — tiresome things. There'll be all kinds of parties, you know." She smiled and turned the ring with her white fingers. "Besides, what could there be about Bernard I don't know?" With the assurance of a woman who knows and wields her power, she gave Arthur a triumphant glance.

Arthur wanted to laugh. Love her, he might. Blinded by her charm, he was not. An unwanted feeling of sympathy went through him. Poor old Bern. If he only realized it, Arthur was doing him a favor. Julia could no more make Bern happy than a pig could fly. His own case offered a whole different story. He knew her for what she was and would, as he'd once told Bern, take his chances. He hid a grin. They had much in common, he and Julia. They both loved her more than anything else in the world.

The self-assurance that had been dampened by news of the engagement and Bern's underhanded way of getting the coveted position returned. All Arthur had to do was to wait for the investigator's report. If nothing turned up in it, so be it. He still had Julia's confidence, friendship, and the feeling he could beat Bern in the courtship game if he had half a chance to be with her more often. He genuinely regretted Mr. Clifton's accident and stroke. Still, a fellow had to take advantage of life's unexpected turns, and this one had given Arthur what he needed most of all: time to become necessary to Julia's happiness.

A haze of love and busy days followed for Bern and Arthur. Like stars in their separate courses, they moved and worked and studied, seldom meeting, never speaking. Weeks dwindled into days. Graduation rushed toward them. Bern's father still could not speak. He made his needs known by writing them down. He never referred to Bern's engagement. On advice of the doctor, Bern did not speak of it. He had taken his father to the finest specialist in Philadelphia, but the eminent doctor discovered little more than the one who first examined him.

"Just don't push him," he advised. "Let him work through things at his own speed."

Bern found himself too busy to do anything else. At Julia's insistence, he did all the things attendant upon him, class dinners, luncheons, teas. Exams ended. Posted grades showed him summa cum laude and first in the class.

Arthur's temporary lapse from his studies resulted in his earning magna cum laude status and second place. He hid his chagrin from even his closest friends with a shrug and lifted eyebrow. "Don't forget. He who laughs last really does laugh best." They wondered at it and he merely grinned. If at times he felt like the protagonist of Robert Louis Stevenson's famous story, no one knew but him. The world saw a calm, engaging Dr. Jekyll. Inside him, Mr. Hyde's fires of revenge blazed. Every careless reference to Bern's luck and success flayed him. He longed for the time he could topple the mighty and told himself he'd have no remorse. Bern had brought it on himself by not playing the game squarely.

Several visits to the investigator disclosed nothing. Then, hours before the medical school's graduation, a messenger summoned Arthur, who dropped everything and hurried to his hireling's chamber, his soul aflame. His knees felt weak. His stomach churned. Surely the investigator wouldn't have sent for him unless he had discovered something.

Arthur reached the office and stopped, strangely hesitant to enter. He could still turn back. A vision of Julia as he'd last seen her strengthened him. For better or worse, he must know what lay waiting beyond the door. He slowly turned the knob.

Chapter 3

Arthur Baldwin took a deep breath, held and released it, then stepped into the office. He faced the sharp-eyed investigator and his throat constricted.

"Well?"

The single word barked like a rifle shot in the stuffy room. Through the telltale cloud of pipe smoke came the victorious reply, "We've got him." One hand slowly clenched. "Right there." The investigator, who sat with his feet on his desk, handed over his report.

Arthur read the few, condemning words. His face turned ashen. All his wildest expectations hadn't come close to the message written in these scrawled lines. For a moment he thought he would faint. He dropped to a chair and stared at the investigator.

"It can't be true," he hoarsely said.

"It is."

"You are sure?"

"I know my business." A puff of smoke rose and partially obscured the man's face.

"Who knows about — this?" Arthur held the page as though it were a coiled rattlesnake ready to spray poisonous venom.

"You. Me. My contact. The Cliftons." Another puff of smoke went up.

"Not Bern." Arthur's voice rang.

"I wouldn't know. What are you going to do with the information you wanted so badly?"

Arthur crumpled the paper into his pocket and didn't answer. After long moments, he placed several large bills on the desk with shaking fingers. "None of your business. Keep your mouth shut and see that your contact does the same."

"Say, who do you think you are?" The man's feet came down with a crash and he scowled. "You're the one who set me on the trail. It's pretty clear you bit off a chaw a lot bigger than you expected. Spit it out or swallow it, makes no difference to me. Just don't stand there telling me how to run my business. As far as blabbing, I'd be out of work if I told the stuff I find out."

"You will be if you ever tell anyone about this!" Arthur shouted and stormed out with a mighty bang of the door.

"Queer duck. Blamed if he isn't the

52

sickest, sorriest looking critter I ever saw." The investigator parked his feet on his desk again and greedily counted his bonus. Baldwin couldn't say he hadn't gotten his money's worth. One raised eyebrow betrayed more curiosity than the investigator had felt in months. A man named Bernard Clifton had one ugly surprise in store for him.

Arthur stumbled from the office and down the street as if pursued by wolves. Never in his life had he felt so unclean or ashamed. He set his fine lips together and passionately wished he had never hired the pipe-smoking investigator. By the time he reached his lodgings, his mind had cleared a bit. He buried the message under piles of clothing in his armoire. If only he could so easily bury the knowledge! As he dressed for the graduation exercises he and Bern had once joyously anticipated, he struggled against good and evil. He could tear up the piece of paper. In spite of his dislike of the human hound, he felt reasonably sure the investigator would keep still. Not from any sense of scruples, but, as he had said, to do differently meant risking his lucrative business.

A new thought came. *Did Bern know?*

"No," Arthur cried to his agonized

mirror image. He furiously brushed his blond mane. "All these years, he couldn't have kept it from me." He had never been more certain of anything. The next instant, a tilted, laughing face came to mind. Julia. It left him weak-kneed and trembling. Julia, who had sighed and said she might care, were it not for Bern. Beneath that stack of clothes lay the means to vanquish his foe forever. Appalled at the very idea of such a betrayal, Arthur dropped his hairbrush and it clattered to the floor. Surely he wasn't cur enough to tell her? *She has the right to know,* the tempter whispered in his ear.

Arthur tore from the room but could not escape his churning thoughts. It took all the self-control and discipline medical training had drummed into him to sit through graduation, his hands clenched to hide their shaking. He caught Bern's glance of amazement that changed to concern. *Did his perturbation show so clearly?* He forced a smile, a poor thing of its kind but enough to get by, and concentrated on the exercises.

Arthur had returned to normalcy enough to experience a thrill of pride when he received his award for high scholastic achievement and loud applause came.

Envy replaced it when a stronger wave of clapping greeted Bern's honors. If the gathered assembly only knew what he did. Arthur forced his attention back to the graduation. His heart swelled and his handsome head proudly lifted. He felt color flow back into his face. His hands steadied. No man had a right to call himself so unless he conquered himself. He would rise above the desire to use sordidness to down his competitor. Joy at self-mastery swelled inside him. He gave Bern a blinding smile, the first in more than a year.

When the other looked startled, then smiled back, Arthur rejoiced. *I'm a better man than you, Bernard Clifton,* he silently exulted. *I have the power to destroy you, but I won't. I'm returning good for evil. You used foul means to get the position we both wanted. I won't stoop so low.*

A pang of regret that Bern would never know dimmed some of the radiance in Arthur's heart, but he stubbornly clung to the high road and told himself he, not the other man, was the real winner in the game.

Yet the minute graduation ended, Julia Langley fluttered up to where the class had assembled outdoors. Never had she been

55

more desirable than in the pale blue she so often wore. Dainty and small, every blond curl in place, she clapped gloved hands in front of her filmy gown with its tiny embroidered rosebuds that matched the sheaf of flowers she carried. Before she gave the bouquet to her fiancé, she smiled alluringly at Arthur.

"Choose one for yourself. Bernard doesn't need them all."

Jealousy swept through Arthur. He fumbled and selected a rose no redder than the drop of blood that appeared on his hand when he encountered a hidden thorn. *What had honor and nobleness of purpose to do with a man's passion for a woman?* He must have Julia, no matter how high the cost.

She has the right to know, the tempter whispered again. *Tell her. If she loves him, it will make no difference.*

Ah, but it would, Arthur knew. The words on the hidden piece of paper blazed red and danced in the air before him. He drew in a long, quivering breath. In spite of everything, he could not bear to see Bern shattered. And what of the white-haired man who had treated Arthur as a second son? Once the news broke, so would Bern's faith in his father.

Could he protect Julia without wrecking the Cliftons' lives? Suppose he told her and swore her to silence. Arthur shook his head. She didn't have it in her not to chatter. He knew beyond a doubt she would never believe Bern guiltless. She'd feel insulted and betrayed and would broadcast her indignation like a sower scattering seed. How would it affect the fine hospital position? Arthur's heart leaped. He knew only too well who was second in line for that job.

Arthur continued to fight his feelings while exchanging courtesies with those who came to congratulate. Was it really a battle about nobility? Or did he merely struggle between divided loyalties? To whom did he owe the most? A friend who had undermined him and won job and girl? Or that same girl who frankly confessed only the interloper stood in the way of Arthur winning her heart and hand? His own heart pounded at the thought. He had to find a way to smash the engagement. Yet a shred of decency simply didn't allow him to go straight to Julia with his hard-bought evidence.

"Congratulations, boys." A warmly smiling Professor Langley appeared, arms outstretched to his two top students. Arthur sagged with relief, his problem solved.

He would give the message to the professor and wash his hands of the whole dirty business. To his mind came the distant memory of a Roman governor who had done the same long ago and discovered he could not so lightly throw off responsibility. Arthur shrugged. He was no Pilate and Bern Clifton certainly no Jesus Christ. Yet the similarity of the situations haunted him, and he decided to forego making a move until at least the next day.

The capricious finger of fate in the person of Julia Langley again changed Arthur's course. Professor Langley had momentarily kidnapped Bern, leaving Julia and Arthur alone. She glanced furtively about, then dimpled up at him. "I have a little present for you. Come." She lightly ran through a nearby rose arbor.

He followed the flutter of her gauzy blue skirt.

As soon as they were away from possible prying eyes, Julia said, "Close your eyes and don't peek."

Tense and wondering, Arthur obeyed. The next instant he felt soft lips pressed against his own, softer than dew on spring grass.

"Julia!" He opened his eyes and reached for her.

She backed away, eyes filled with mischief. "No, Arthur."

"You care for me," he cried in a hoarse, intense voice. "You can't marry anyone else."

"Of course I can, silly." She relented enough to say, "I'm sorry if I hurt you. You know how fond I am of you. I thought you'd want something to remember me by." Her eyes glistened.

Righteous indignation rose within Arthur. For the third and final time, the tempter's voice came. *She has the right to know.*

"You will never marry Bern," he hoarsely told her. "And one day you will thank me for saving you." He turned on his heel and ran the way he had done from the investigator's office. He ignored Julia's plea for him to come back and strode on, away from her and everything but the need to act. Now.

Straight to his lodgings he went. He jumbled the neat stack of clothing and retrieved the incontrovertible evidence and pocketed it. White with determination, Arthur made his way to the Langley residence. When the professor returned home, having chosen to walk rather than ride in the family carriage, he found a white-faced man awaiting him in the library.

"Why, Arthur! What is it? Surely not Julia." Professor Langley's face blanched at the thought. "I just left her."

"Not what you think, sir, but it is about Julia."

"Sit down, son." The professor took a chair across from his guest and sighed. "I know you're in love with her, but there's nothing I can do. You and Bernard Clifton are both fine young men. One was bound to win, the other lose. She's chosen him and it's irrevocable. My wife has the wedding all but planned —"

"I have evidence that puts him beyond the pale as a suitable husband for your daughter. I also believe she cares for me."

Professor Langley drew himself up. His eyes flashed. "Really, Baldwin, aren't you being presumptuous? I find nothing whatsoever in Clifton to warrant such a charge. I am disappointed that you'd lower yourself to such tactics. I've been aware of Julia's flirtations, but this is unbelievable."

Arthur felt hot blood pour into his face. "I have proof." He fumbled in his pocket, took out the report, and handed it to the professor.

With a look of contempt, the older man read the message. His face changed to disbelief, anger, and fear. "Where on earth did you get such an infamous piece of nonsense, anyway?" His voice shook and lines engraved themselves in his scholarly face.

"You'll note it's from one of Philadelphia's leading investigators," Arthur said in an unsteady voice.

"You'll vouch for its truth?" Great drops of sweat sprang to the professor's forehead.

"The investigator staked his honor and business on the authenticity of the report."

"How did it come into your hands?" The question sounded loud and accusing in the quiet room, although the professor had spoken barely above a whisper.

"I love your daughter, to the point of using fair means or foul to win her." Wounds from old grievances at Bern's hands rose to justify Arthur's actions. "After Julia told me how Bern got the hospital job, not on his merits but through her influence, I decided I might as well play the same game."

"Neither Clifton nor I knew her intentions. Julia took advantage of a long-term friendship and rushed in where she had no business interfering."

Arthur felt sick. He had mentally based much of his own defense on Bern's departure from the sportsmanship they had always observed. "She told me —" He clamped his mouth shut, not daring to tell the professor his daughter had lied. Or had she merely allowed him to interpret the situation incorrectly?

"I regret to admit it, but Julia sees life as she wants to and repeats it that way." The professor's voice confirmed his suspicions.

A wave of remorse washed through Arthur Baldwin until he felt he would drown in its depths. He had betrayed his friend — for what? Not thirty pieces of silver as Judas did Christ, but for the hand of a woman incapable of really loving anyone but herself. The scales dropped from his eyes, and with them, his infatuation. He stared at the professor, remembering little things. Julia, feeding his vanity by plaintively hinting at what might have been in order to keep him among her admirers. Julia, offering just enough so he wouldn't slip through her greedy, useless fingers. Julia, giving him pick of the bouquet of roses, a kiss that rightly belonged to Bern. His hands clenched.

"God forgive me," he choked out. "What have I done?" Yet even through his Gethsemane, Arthur found himself giving thanks. Scurrilous as his deed had been, it meant Bern would be free of a loveless marriage.

Laughing voices rang in the hall: Julia's high, sweet treble, Mrs. Clifton's mature, even tones, Bern's deep laugh.

Arthur cringed. For a single craven moment he considered leaping from a window in order to avoid what lay ahead.

Did the professor sense his guest's cowardice? A scathing look nailed Arthur to the chair. The door swung open and the trio swept inside.

"Why, Arthur, how nice of you to come!" Julia trilled.

Arthur wanted to curse her, to hold up her inner falseness that had destroyed him and would soon crush the best friend he ever had. Iron entered his soul, but he could not utter a single word.

"Run along, dear. You, too, Julia," the professor ordered. "I want to speak with Bernard." Arthur marveled that the only sign of his distress lay in his tightly clasped hands and white knuckles.

"Really, Father. Must you talk business now?" Her blue gaze drifted between the three men in a measuring look, then she went out, leaving the door slightly ajar.

"Close the door tightly and take a chair, if you will, Bernard."

Bern complied, looking bewildered.

Arthur ached for Bern, so tall, straight, and fine. He wondered if he could keep the gorge inside him from rising long enough to make it through the coming interview. He longed to fall on his knees and ask forgiveness, then scorned the thought. A man who had done what he did deserved no pardon.

"Something unpleasant has come to my attention," the professor quietly said. "Now, before we discuss it, I want you to know that nothing on earth can alter my admiration for you, Bernard. However, what I am about to disclose can and will change the circumstances for — all of us." His voice wobbled and he drew forth a handkerchief and mopped his brow.

"I don't understand," Bern quietly spoke.

"Tell me, what do you know about your mother?"

"Why, just that she died when I was born. Father brought me up." Bern looked more and more confused.

"An investigator has discovered other things." The professor glanced at the piece of paper in his lap, swallowed, and tried to speak. When no words came, he handed it to Bern.

In one quick glance, the tall medical man scanned the words. His face turned to ashes, then flames.

"Where did you get this wicked lie?" He swung toward Arthur and his eyes narrowed to slits. "You?" Disbelief changed to red rage.

Arthur sat stonelike. "Yes."

Bern's pent-up fury exploded into a pantherlike leap that carried him, his victim, and the chair to the floor with a horrid crash. His great fist rose and fell with deadly accuracy. Blood spurted from the first blow. The second.

"Clifton, stop this at once!"

Professor Langley's plea and the terrible jerk he gave to his student's shoulders went unheeded. Bern struck again and again. He continued the relentless punishment until Arthur lay still, never realizing the blond-haired man had made no attempt to either defend himself or stop the attack.

He staggered to his feet. His ears rang. Sanity slowly returned.

"You've killed him!" the professor wailed. "Clifton, you've killed him!"

Bern shook his head, knelt, and felt for a pulse. "He's not dead, though he ought to be."

A pounding came at the door. "Father?"

65

"Stay out of here," he ordered, but too late.

The door swung open. Julia stepped inside. Her gaze fixed in fascinated horror on Arthur, his blood-covered face beaten beyond recognition. She screamed wildly and threw her hands into the air.

"What have you done?" she accused Bern.

"It's not what I have done," he retorted, stung that in the horrible moment her loyalties lay elsewhere. "He lied and —"

"That's enough!" The professor furiously rang for Thomas. "Get out, Julia, and stay out." Something in her father's voice sent Julia crying from the room, but not until she had given Bern a look that killed something inside him. No matter what the future held, he could never again see her as one far above the world and its passions. That one look had betrayed her.

Thomas came on the run, glanced down, and shook his head. "Bad business, this. Mr. Baldwin needs a doctor, bad."

"Let me." Bern started to examine the damages he had inflicted.

"Can I trust you?" The professor's cold voice snapped him to attention.

"I am a doctor, sir." He bent to his task, the professor and Thomas alert to his every move. "Broken nose. No other lasting damage."

"Clifton, you are a savage!" Professor Langley's contempt stung like a swarm of angry bees. "If you have no more control than this, I suggest you get out of medicine, for the good of the patients — and yourself," he added significantly.

"I will never do that." Bern expertly patched up his limp enemy.

"Man, he never raised a hand, all during your beating!" the professor spat out.

Bern's head jerked up. "I don't believe it."

"Look at yourself. You're without a scratch."

For a heartbeat Bern returned to another time. His first year in college Arthur Baldwin had taken a licking without defending himself. "I deserved it for cheating," he'd said through swollen lips after his friend had chastised him. The memory convinced Bern. He suddenly felt sick. *How could the inert man have given him that brilliant comradely smile when he knew that within the hour he would betray? Indeed, hadn't Judas kissed the Master in the garden?*

On Professor Langley's insistence, they put the still-unconscious Arthur to bed in a spare room.

"I think you had better go now," the professor said frostily. "I will of course investigate the truth of the matter. In the meantime, I suggest you ask your father."

"I wouldn't so insult him!" Bern blazed. His mouth dried at the idea. "In his condition it might kill him."

"He has to know sooner or later if it's true." Some of the antagonism left the professor's face. "Bernard, I pray to God it won't be, but I am terribly afraid. This investigator is known for his expert work. He wouldn't dare report such a monstrous thing unless he were sure."

"Give me the report." Bern held out a blood-stained hand. "I'll go to him and —"

"Beat him to death?" the professor inquired. "I think it best if I go with you."

Two hours later, they left the smoke-filled office. Bern felt he had been tainted both with the haze and the man's assurance he had uncovered the facts.

"I guess I will have to ask Dad," he admitted. Dread underlined every word. "You know I'll believe him, no matter what that pipe-smoker says. Dad's never lied to me."

"Hasn't he?" The professor sounded hostile. "It seems to me, if the report is accurate, your father has been living a lie with you for years."

"It isn't true." Yet doubt blacker than tar crept into the tall young doctor's heart. *Why hadn't he asked Dad more about the mother who died giving life to her tiny son?* He thought back to the few times he'd inquired, the look of deep pain his questions brought. Dad invariably changed the subject and diverted the small boy's attention to other things.

"You know what this means concerning Julia." The flat statement brought Bern out of his wondering. "I will personally continue to have high regard for you, providing of course you don't repeat the performance in my library. I cannot allow you to marry my daughter, however, unless this is a hoax, a false charge trumped up by Arthur Baldwin. Frankly, I don't think even he would go this far unless he were certain. He certainly acted strange today."

The keen gaze bored into his companion.

"He believed you sent Julia to get the job for you. It angered him and he determined to discredit you. The look on his face when he discovered you were innocent of any unethical practice such as that was a revelation. I've never seen such regret in a human face, or such misery. It explains why he didn't strike back."

"Too bad the regret came *after* showing you the report," Bern sneered. "I'm going home to talk with Dad. I'll be over later this evening and clear everything up." He laughed ruefully. "I have the feeling it will take some talking to get me out of trouble with my fiancée!"

"And with her father," the professor ominously warned.

Bern watched the man he admired with heart and soul turn away. He felt like a child abandoned on a cold, lonely doorstep. Then he turned toward home. Dad would be waiting.

Chapter 4

Dad would be waiting.

Bernard Clifton paused, expecting the familiar rush of reassurance that always came when he ran home to his father. Dad never failed to care for childhood hurts or to mend broken toys. Why, then, did Bern's long stride falter and slow to reluctant steps? Surely, he didn't believe the theatrical claptrap of a pipe-smoking snoop in a smoke-filled office! "O ye of little faith," he murmured and charted his course. Dad must never think his only son had for even one second believed the charge to be anything more than a product of Arthur's fertile mind. Bern's lip curled. How much had "Judas" Baldwin paid to make it worth the investigator's while to lie? He had plenty, inherited from ancestors more wealthy than worthwhile, according to Arthur.

Feeling more like himself, Bern produced a whistle and bounded up the steps, across the porch, down the hall, and into his father's room.

"Well, graduation's over and I'm ready for a change."

He flung himself into a chair, noting how his father's eyes brightened at his coming. How should he approach the subject uppermost in his mind? Rush right into it or lead up to it by telling him again about Julia? A pang went through him. Some of her luster had dimmed in the Langley library. Could he ever recapture it? He impatiently brushed the idea aside, knowing it must be dealt with but postponing it until his father denied the monstrous lie that lay cold and heavy in his soul.

"I hate to bother you," he began. Feeling his way, he chose every word carefully.

Bern went on. "You won't believe the lengths to which Arthur Baldwin has gone out of jealousy." He laughed harshly. "I can barely take it in. You know he coveted the hospital position I won. Well, he coveted the girl who promised to marry me, as well. Dad, do you remember I told you about Julia Langley, just before you fell? That she had promised to be my wife?" Wistfulness crept into his voice. If only Dad hadn't forgotten, it would be so much easier.

His father's face whitened. His expression changed to anxiety. The furrows in his face deepened. He raised a hand in an involuntary gesture that looked like one warding off a blow.

Bern nearly dropped the subject. Why trouble Dad, especially when he continued to be so frail? Yet he had to know. The thought blanched his deeply tanned face and made him feel sick. Could he actually be giving credence to the report, at least enough to want it openly and frankly denied? *It's so I have positive proof for the Langleys,* he told himself and knew he lied. More than he'd ever wanted anything on earth, the position, Julia, fame, he longed for truth to blaze in his father's eyes, indignation strong enough to sweep away every wisp of doubt.

Bern slowly took the crumpled report from his pocket. He avoided the other man's gaze. "Arthur hired a private investigator."

The elder Clifton lay as one dead. No sound escaped his pallid lips.

"I'll read it to you." Bern paused. Would the words come from his dry mouth? He took a deep breath and began.

"Seattle, Washington. Investigation shows male child born December 31, 1866. Fa-

73

ther: Reverend Clifton, first name un-known."

"No!" An awful animal cry burst from the invalid, the first word he'd uttered since the fall that resulted in a stroke.

Bern's whole body shook. It took super-human strength not to look at his father. Driven by his own need, he hoarsely read the remainder of the incriminating report. "Mother: Crying Dove, a full-blooded Indian."

"God forgive me, what have I done?" The anguished wail echoed the remorse in Arthur Baldwin's cry a few hours earlier.

The report dropped from nerveless fingers. Bern felt the blood rush from his head, leaving him faint and fighting nausea. He risked a look into the beloved face and groaned aloud.

"That's my birthdate, but this is some other Clifton, isn't it? Dad, tell me it isn't true." Yet he knew it was by the dead-white color of his father's twisted face, even before the older man brokenly nodded.

Bern started to stand. His knees buckled and he collapsed back into his chair. His brain felt numb the way it had when he poured everything he knew into a crucial exam or wracked his mind to diagnose an unusual case.

"So long ago," his father babbled. "The traces of your Indian mother were not readily discernible as such. I thought you need never know." His nervous fingers pleated and unpleated the light bedcovers. His eyes looked more colorless than ever.

"Coward!" The faltering excuse shook Bern into painful, throbbing life. He leaped to his feet and towered over the bed.

"What good would knowing have done you?" his father pleaded. "You'd only have known pain —"

"Pain! You talk of pain? How do you think it feels to be on top of the world and have the whole thing taken from you?" His laugh grated like a dull saw through a gigantic fir. A new thought intruded, one he hadn't given consideration since first reading the report. "It says *Reverend* Clifton. You were a minister?"

"Yes."

It explained so much, especially his violent reaction the day his son jokingly accused him of preaching.

"You, a preacher . . ." He couldn't continue.

His father turned even paler. "I fell in love with Crying Dove the first time she and her father, Chief Running Wolf, came

75

into my church. She was the loveliest creature I'd ever seen and filled with goodness. The chief challenged me and said I didn't talk enough about Jesus. I realized he spoke the truth and I went to the Indian village nearby to apologize." Humility swept over his faith. "God used one I considered a savage to show me how far my preaching fell short of what it should be."

"And you rewarded him by taking his daughter." The ugliness of it all seared Bern like a white-hot poker, leaving scars that could never heal.

Clifton stared at his son and shrank back as if struck. "Not the way you think. I respected Crying Dove. I knew white ministers would never marry us, so we pledged ourselves in an Indian ceremony performed by Chief Running Wolf." A spasm of pain filled his face.

"Someday I'll tell you the whole story, of a man who owed me nothing but silently bore the weight of my actions. For now, it's enough that you know I married Crying Dove as honorably as I could, hoping to one day find an ordained minister to add his blessing. I took her away. You came." His voice turned lifeless. "She died giving birth."

"I trusted you. I knew you'd never do

anything dishonorable," Bern ranted. "Dad, why did you lie to me?"

"I didn't lie. I just didn't tell you everything," his father weakly defended. He closed his eyes and his lips moved, as if in prayer.

Bern's mouth curled in contempt. "Praying won't help you. It won't even make you feel less ashamed."

"Bernard, I regret the actions of a young man who foolishly did something that caused a great deal of pain to others, especially you." The white head proudly came up. "You must believe one thing. I am not ashamed of Crying Dove. If I can be half the Christian she was, I'll be proud and count my life worthy."

"Proud you were a squaw man?" Rage overcame everything except the need to thrust and wound, as he had been wounded.

"Never use that terrible word again!" Some of his father's old spirit raised to glowing life. "You degrade yourself, me, and your mother." His hands trembled when Bern involuntarily flinched. "Yes, your mother. She came from a long and unbroken line of chieftains. Crying Dove was a princess in her tribe. I pray that one day you will proudly accept your heritage." His voice broke.

"If you were so proud of it, you wouldn't have kept it secret for the past twenty-six years," Bern retorted. He started for the door, reached it, and whirled back toward his father. Bitter lines formed around his sensitive mouth. "I'm leaving, Dad."

"Where are you going?"

"Does it matter?" Bern wanted to hurl threats and invectives. He did neither. He simply stood there and grew old before his father's watching eyes. "I owe it to Professor Langley to tell him the truth, that I–I'm a half-breed." He hated the break in his voice, the stinging behind his eyes. "He will never consent to letting Julia marry me now." Hopelessness filled him.

"If she truly loves you, she will cling to you in spite of everything," Clifton quietly told his son.

A gleam of hope twinkled like a firefly in darkness. The next instant a rush of certainty drowned it. "She won't. She'll accept Arthur Baldwin. I hope the two of them live miserably ever after."

"Doesn't she at least deserve the chance to decide?"

Again the firefly of hope flickered. Bern shook his head. "I don't know."

"Your mother would have followed me to the ends of the earth and gone gladly."

The comment toppled the precarious pile of burdens on Bern's back. "My mother was an Indian, remember?" He bolted from the room, feeling pursued by more troubles than any man should bear. Yet a short while later, dressed and polished to perfection, he presented himself at the Langley mansion.

Thomas opened the door as usual. This time, however, he wore no friendly smile but a dour expression that foreboded little welcome. Thomas was not in the habit of having gentleman callers beat other guests senseless in the Langley mansion.

"I'd like to see Professor Langley."

"Very well. Wait here, please." He omitted the word *sir*.

Bern inwardly squirmed and vowed again never to have a haughty butler who made callers uncomfortable. He watched Thomas majestically march down the long hall. An eternity later he reappeared, still frowning his disapproval. In dead silence he ushered Bern into a formal waiting room. Five minutes later an unsmiling Professor Langley entered, waved Bern to a seat, and took a chair across from him.

"Well?"

"It's true."

Every vestige of color left the professor's

face. "I wished before God it were not. What are you going to do about it?"

"With or without your permission, I intend to tell Julia the truth and let her decide whether she wishes to continue with our engagement." Bern spoke calmly, as if discussing a medical problem. The walk in the fresh evening air had restored his self-control and armed him for the coming unpleasantness he knew he could expect.

Angry red sped to the professor's cheeks. "You think she will for one minute allow it to stand, even if in a fit of nobility and madness I consented?"

"She is of age. She has a right to know and to decide for herself."

The professor leaned forward, genuine regret showing in his stiffened body. "I am sorry for you, Bernard. I beg of you, don't expose yourself to further humiliation by seeking an interview with my daughter."

"I must." He clenched his hands. "Professor, if it were you, wouldn't you —"

"I would. I only want to spare you. You see, I know Julia."

The warning sent splinters of ice into Bern, but he only said, "I hope I may see her with your permission."

For a long, measuring moment his former mentor and father-in-law-to-be scanned him in a look Bernard Clifton would never forget. "You may." He rose heavily and extended a hand. "You realize that should she consent, which she will not, it means ostracism from everyone and everything she has known."

He found himself parroting his father's words. "If she really loves me, she will accept that, great as it is to ask. Perhaps her world will lay aside prejudice after I begin my new position."

A shadow dropped over Professor Langley's face. He started to speak and stopped. "I'll send Julia in."

She came in a flurry of new-April green, flounced and ruffled. "Bernard?" She hesitated in the doorway before entering.

He saw unforgiveness in her face but no trace of shock. "I came to apologize for offending you, even though Arthur —"

"What you did was unspeakable. Father says Arthur never raised a hand to defend himself," she coldly cut in.

Bern had the feeling she'd been iced and frozen. Even anger would be better, he decided. "Do you know he hired a private investigator to see if he could dig up something to discredit me with you?" he flared.

"Really?" Warmth flowed back into her

beautiful, shallow face. "Do sit down and tell me about it. Why, I didn't know he cared so much."

To Bern's amazement, she actually looked pleased. One more illusion about her purity and innocence died, but Bern manfully struggled on. "Arthur's jealousy led to it," he explained.

"Well, did he find anything?" she flippantly asked. One hand pulled a long curl over her white shoulder and she toyed with it.

The same fierce desire to shake her out of her indifference that had caused him to act rashly in the past caused him to say, "Just that I'm half Indian."

"How droll." She laughed merrily and her pearl-like teeth shone between parted pink lips. "Anything else?"

Relief made him stagger. "You mean it doesn't make any difference?"

She surveyed him from shining black hair to highly polished shoe tips. "Why should such a story make a difference?" She cocked her pretty head. "You don't look nearly as Indianlike as you did in college when you were out playing ball in the sun."

Her words sank into a mind that had bounced from mountain to valley and back to hilltop during the day. "I'm not pretending, Julia. I learned this afternoon for the first time that the mother who died giving me life was an Indian girl Father married in Seattle."

Her eyes grew enormous. Her face lost its delicate color.

"Need it make a difference, dearest? If you love me —" He dropped to his knees and attempted to take her hands.

"No!" Julia scrambled from her chair in the fastest movement he'd ever seen her make. "Don't touch me," she gasped. "How could you think I'd marry you now?" She looked at him as if he repelled her. "No decent woman would even consider such a thing. What would my friends say?"

For the second time in the same day, another of Julia Langley's suitors saw her as she really was. Bern stood for a moment, noting the loathing in her face.

Maddened by his stare, she cried, "Go! Now!" Her voice rose to a hysterical note and she flung the door open. "Father, send this impostor away! I never want to see him again!" She ran out in a flutter of green draperies.

The professor led Bern to the door and opened it. "I believe you have your answer.

Good-bye, Bernard, and God help you. I don't know anyone else who can." He sounded old and tired.

"God?" Bern stepped back as if the word were foreign to him. "What kind of god lets a man rise to the heights and be flung down in his moment of highest achievement? Some capricious being who taunts mortals by allowing them a glimpse of heaven before shoving them into torment?"

He blindly rushed into the growing night. His feet instinctively turned toward home before the growing realization he had no home overwhelmed him. He made an about-face and climbed to the high point that looked down on the City of Brotherly Love. How ironic! He didn't know one person in that city who would continue to admire him once the truth came out.

"And it will," he grimly told the rising night wind. "Julia will spread the news. Her cohorts will commiserate with her and she'll enjoy every minute of the notoriety."

Newspaper headlines wrote themselves in his mind. DAUGHTER OF NOTED PROFESSOR NARROWLY ESCAPES MARRYING A HALF-BREED. Or, PRIVATE INVESTIGATION BY CONCERNED SUITOR PAYS OFF.

The longing to escape seized Bern by the throat. *Why not pack a few clothes and simply get away, at least for a time?* He stared down on the lighted windows and shook his head. He couldn't go. If he left now, it meant giving up the position he'd aimed for ever since he heard of it. It also meant handing the plum over to Arthur.

"Never! I won't flee. I'll stay and fight," he vowed. "I'll show them all. I won't leave until I become the finest surgeon in this city. I'll move on to New York and do the same." He shook his fist at the clustered stars that looked down on him. "I can't control the past, but no one else is going to control my future. Not a woman or Dad or God, if there is one after all. Let Arthur and his ilk have the Julias of the world. I'll travel alone and make Dr. Bernard Clifton's name so famous it won't matter what he is or where he came from."

The night wind moaned like something in pain and sent a chill down Bern's back, but he shook his fist again and laughed into the ever-darkening night. Spent but strangely at peace, he started down the hill. All his fine plans made on the mountaintop had to be carried out in the valley below. As he walked, one by one the yellow lamplighted squares grew dark. He laughed and called himself superstitious for seeing anything symbolic in those black windows. Still, he couldn't recapture his high spirits.

Even the well-lighted Clifton home failed to cheer him. Tomorrow he had to tell Dad he was leaving, for good. How could a man so betrayed be expected to forgive? Yet without forgiveness, they could not live together. His father's presence would be a constant reminder of what lay between them. Unspoken recriminations and corroding bitterness could become hatred. Bern shrank from the idea. He did not want to hate Dad. Better to make a clean, sharp break. He avoided going to his father's room when he got home and fell asleep the moment he tumbled into bed.

The next morning, Mr. Clifton walked to the breakfast table. Had his returning speech brought energy with it? He carried his Bible. Bern idly wondered if it had brought the look of peace he wore. Bern resented that look. How dare Dad appear fresher than he had been in weeks while his son inwardly bled to death!

Clifton introduced the subject on Bern's mind after breakfast. "I assume your engagement is broken or you would have told me when you came in."

"Thanks to you." He gathered up the dirty dishes.

"Bernard, when you take your new position, you need to live elsewhere. I believe our only hope of reconciliation lies in our being apart." He smiled sadly when a dish crashed to the floor and his son stood as if paralyzed.

"Just now you're still reeling from Arthur's treachery and Miss Langley's rejection, as well as my silence and news of your mother. You feel it is impossible to forgive. Yet haven't you shaken your head over a badly fractured bone, only to see it knit and heal, often stronger than before? Consider this. The day you are able to forgive me will be the day our relationship becomes stronger than ever because it is based on full truth."

"How can you sit there talking of forgiveness?" Bern burst out. "What do you know about how I feel?"

His father held up the Bible. "For years I have sought God's forgiveness. Early this morning I confessed my inability to receive what I knew was there all along. I am free, Bernard, free *because I have chosen freedom.* I cannot change the past, but I refuse to be crippled by it any longer. If it weren't for your suffering, I would get down on my knees and give thanks to God the secret is out!"

Bern had never seen him so impassioned. He thought of his own vigil on the hilltop the night before. It paralleled his father's thoughts. "Dad, I —"

His father spoke at the same time and drowned out the fragile beginning. "When do you start at the hospital?"

"I told them two weeks after graduation. They can probably use me sooner now that I'm free." Excitement rose within him and he actually smiled. "I think I'll drop by this morning and see."

"Good for you. I feel so much better I'm going to tackle some of the chores."

Bern's professional training made him warn, "Don't overdo it."

"I won't." His voice sounded strange. "Bernard, if other things prove to be disappointing, can you handle it?"

"What other things?" His stomach churned, but his father waved him away.

"Go on to your appointment and don't listen to an old doomsayer."

All the way across town to the imposing hospital, Bern wondered. He gave his name to a human watchdog outside the director's office who trotted into the inner sanctum and came out with a brief, "They're waiting for you. Go right in."

They? Caught aback by the messenger's words, Bern stepped into the office. He'd been there for his final interview and determined to have one just like it, from the rich burgundy carpet to paintings by the old masters. The hospital director sat behind a carved, dark desk. Five other doctors Bern recognized from his hospital tour occupied plush chairs. At the director's wave, he took the last empty one.

"Glad you stopped by, Clifton. We were just discussing the final selection for our opening." The hospital director neither offered his hand nor smiled.

"Final selection? I received written notification to report for duty the middle of this month." Bern stared directly at the cold-eyed doctor. Where was the affable man who nodded his pleasure during the extensive interview?

"The notice was sent prematurely. In the light of — that is, further consideration has shown another doctor to be even more qualified for this particular position: Arthur Baldwin. I believe you know him."

Bern glanced from him to each of the others in turn. Three looked flint-hard, one squirmed, and the fifth refused to meet his gaze. He rose, towering over the men who had become his enemies.

"You lie and you know it." He threw back his head. "I stood at the head of my class."

"We have other qualifications, a professional image to maintain." The director also rose. "Leave it at that and go."

"I will *not* leave it at that." Bern set his jaw and folded his arms. "I'm staying until you tell me what this is all about and show cause to explain your withdrawal of my appointment."

Chapter 5

For a full moment no one spoke. At last the hospital director asked, "Did or did you not attack a man in Professor Langley's home and beat him severely? The same man competing for the job, once your friend?"

"I did. I'd do it again. He behaved execrably and got what he deserved. No man can —"

"Please, Clifton. Spare us your whining." A careless hand cut him off.

All the anger and bitterness of betrayal exploded. In a mighty leap, Bern cleared the distance between them and leaned across the desk. Although he didn't touch the director, the man's face turned pasty and he shoved his great chair back. A low murmur came from the others. Bern's black gaze raced from face to face. Suspicion rose. In a flash he understood the odd look Professor Langley had given him when Bern spoke of taking the position and becoming acceptable.

Another thought followed close on the first suspicion's heels — his father wondering if he could handle more disappointment. Everything fell into place: the meeting of the hospital's crowned heads; the look on the watchdog clerk's face; the contempt he'd felt when he stepped inside the room; even the director's refusal to offer his hand.

"Why don't you have the guts to come out with it?" he sneered. "This has nothing to do with what I did to Baldwin. You're simply refusing to hire a half-breed, aren't you?" Bern knew he had scored. "What do you think I'm going to do? Go on the warpath, scalp some of you?" He laughed in their alarmed faces.

"I told you we have an image to maintain." Sweat broke out on the director's face. "Miss Langley recognizes that. We are deeply indebted to her for having the courage to step forward and warn us of the violent temper of the doctor we planned to add to our staff."

"It's no more than I expected." Bern coolly surveyed the assembled group. "Now, what are you going to do about breaching your contract?"

"There's not a court in the land that

won't uphold our decision," one of the other doctors put in. "Better leave it and get out while you can, Clifton."

"If you don't, you'll never practice medicine in Philadelphia or anywhere else," the hospital director threatened.

Bern opened his mouth to cry out for them to do their worst. He'd never touch an instrument again, anyway. But just before he spoke, he remembered his promise to his father. He shriveled his enemies with a lightning glance and yanked open the door. Before it closed behind him, he heard one of the doctors say, "He may be half-Indian, but by all that's holy, he's all man!"

Bern laughed mockingly. So he had left a mark. Good. Someday those six smug doctors would read of his exploits and remember this day. He slammed the door as loudly as its well-oiled hinges would allow. The bang wilted the watchdog into a whipped pup in the corner. Bern sent him a look of disgust. *How could a man allow himself to become a lackey, fetching and carrying on command?* Wait. *Isn't that what he'd have become if Julia had married him?* He rejected the idea, but it returned with all its companions. He tried to tell himself it wouldn't have happened but failed miserably.

"Maybe I should send Arthur a letter of condolence," he said aloud and stepped outdoors. He inhaled and exhaled deeply to expel some of the poison left by the interview. *Why worry on a day like this?* He was young, qualified, and ready for the next opportunity on the list of places that had clamored for his skills before they discovered he'd been selected for the other job. Three disgruntled directors had even offered him more money and a free hand. Which should he try first? He doubted any of the positions had been filled. With his credentials, he'd have no trouble getting selected.

Three interviews later, he discovered how sadly mistaken he'd been. Too proud to march under false colors, Bern reminded the three how they had found him almost too good to be true. He bluntly stated he had since learned he was half-Indian. Blank stares greeted him in two cases before the interviewers shook their heads and mumbled excuses no eight-year-old would believe. He gave each an icy stare guaranteed to remain with them and walked out.

The third doctor at least treated him fairly. "Clifton, I'd give anything to hire you and I'd do it on the spot. Wouldn't do a bit of good, though. Word's around and our board's already stated that if you approach me, I have to show you the door." He grinned. "Some chance. If you don't mind listening to an old codger, I'll give you a piece of advice." He leaned forward and laced his fingers. "Get away from Philadelphia and this whole snobbish East Coast. Go somewhere and find folks who don't know you and won't give a hang, so long as you take care of them. California, maybe. Or Washington — it's just getting used to being a state."

"Not Washington." Bern ground his teeth.

The doctor raised a shaggy eyebrow. "How about another country?"

"I'd like to stay in the United States," Bern said slowly. "Don't ask me why, but I never see a flag without wanting to take off my hat and cheer." His face burned. Why had he opened his heart to this stranger?

"Don't apologize for that," the doctor barked. "So do I. Say, if I were thirty years younger and didn't have a family, I'd head north." His eyes glistened. "Blamed if I wouldn't see something of Canada, then end up in Alaska Territory. Plenty of elbow room there and only a handful of doctors. Think of it. A medical practice that encompasses five hundred, maybe a thousand miles. Small towns where people die when they don't need to. Son, you could be busy twenty-five hours a day. I envy you." His keen gaze searched Bern's face. "You're young and you've had a bad disappointment. Well, I've heard it said the Almighty is a whole lot more interested in what we do with our troubles than in the troubles themselves." His weary face shadowed. "Don't let a false friend and a pretty little fluffy-ruffles give you the idea your life's over." He grinned. "Sure, I've heard the story *and* the sequel. Did you know Dr. Baldwin flatly refused the job you were ousted from?"

Bern jerked upright. "Why? Couldn't he stand being second choice?"

"You know him better than I do." The interviewing doctor shrugged massive shoulders. His eyes twinkled. "How am I doing as a gossip?"

"How do you know so much?"

"Professor Langley and I've been friends for years. You may not believe it now, but he thinks a lot of you. By the way," he added a shade too casually, "according to him, Baldwin moved out the minute he could and hasn't been back. Miss Langley sent him several invitations to visit and he politely wrote back that after considering all that had happened, he felt it best not to intrude on the Langleys' lives. Said he'd done you a grave injustice and that he planned to go away and find a job in a hospital as far from Philadelphia as he could get."

A tiny feeling of warmth nibbled at the icy chunk of resentment inside Bern. "What did the professor say? Seeing you're doing so well at gossip."

"He up and told Miss Langley she let the two finest men she'd ever meet slip away because of her flirting and he only regretted not getting one or the other as a son-in-law!"

The doctor laughed out loud, glanced at his watch, and exclaimed, "I'm late for a consultation. Good luck, Clifton." His huge paw shot out. "Drop me a line someday from Alaska?"

"Am I going there?" Bern could feel a smile lurking behind his lips.

"I wouldn't be at all surprised." The doctor hurried him out, let his heavy hand fall on the younger man's shoulder, and then trotted off to his delayed appointment. His open discussion of the situation and helpful suggestions gave Bern much to consider, especially the part about Arthur.

Chapter 6

Anastasia Jeanne Anton wholeheartedly and unreservedly fell in love on May 1, 1898, her twenty-third birthday. Her fur trader father, Nicolai, known as "White Father" to the Indians in Tarnigan near the Endicott Mountains of north central Alaska, laughed until his great frame shook.

"So, Little Flower, he has captured your heart!"

Sparkles like sun on the icicles that hung on *Nika Illahee* (Chinook for "my dear homeland") in winter brightened Sasha's slightly slanted brown eyes. Twin braids of wavy dark hair, tied with red ribbons and half as thick as her father's brawny wrist hung in front of her slim, sturdy shoulders. Wild rose petals of excitement touched the white skin inherited from her French mother and blended beautifully with her father's Russian-Indian heritage.

"Should I be jealous?" Blond-haired

Ivan Romanov's drawl sounded out of keeping with his frank face. Both hid the shrewd business ability for which Nicolai had hired him to manage the Anton trading post and fur business.

"Don't be silly, Ivan," Sasha imperiously told him. "Father, you can't imagine how glad I am you brought him. He's the best birthday present in the world."

The object of her adoration smiled a lazy grin and licked Sasha's fingers with an eager pink tongue. His plumy tail curled over his back.

A flash of the jealousy Ivan mentioned crept into his eyes. Never in the four years since he came to Tarnigan and fell in love with nineteen-year-old Sasha had she looked at him the way she did at the malamute pup. Never had she hugged him or put her lips to his face. His face burned at the thought. The few times he'd made the mistake of attempting a caress, she reproved him with a glance, patted his arm, and raced away.

Anger and desire filled him. Sasha Anton was one of two reasons he stayed in Tarnigan. He'd made himself indispensable to her father and taken the place of the brother she never had. Someday, the second reason would no longer exist.

When that happened, he intended to marry Sasha and take her far away from this top of the world outpost. Visions of cities and tall buildings rose in his mind. Beautiful as she was in the deerskins and parkas and the simple gowns she donned in the house, Sasha would shine brighter than the aurora borealis in silks and satins of his choosing. He remembered other women, perfumed and alluring. His lip curled in contempt. Bah, not one of them could match the child of the wild he'd discovered here in Tarnigan, just a few miles from the Arctic Circle.

"Isn't he beautiful?" the girl crooned. She raised the pup's front paws until he stood on his back legs. Dark gray and white with a white chest and face, the darker markings on his face made him look like he wore a mask. "Ivan, did you notice? His eyes are the same shade of blue as yours. They look like the heart of a glacier."

Ivan snorted. "Thank you very much, Miss Anton." His nostrils flared with disgust. "It's bad enough that you can't see anything but the mutt without comparing his eyes to mine."

"He's not a mutt." She hugged the puppy and gloated. Her naturally red lips parted in an enchanting smile. "He's going to be the best sled dog in Alaska. Just wait and see."

Nicolai roared with delight. "She has you there, Romanov. This pup is pick of the litter with good blood behind him. With proper training, he can become a champion — just like the Antons." All the love he'd known for the wife who died giving birth to his child shone from his dark eyes along with the pride of his heritage.

"Now, Father, don't bore Ivan with family history." Sasha pulled her chin in toward her chest and intoned in a fair imitation of Nicolai, "Do we not have a right to be proud? Are we not descendants of Alexander Baranof himself, first manager of the Russian-American Company, a trading firm and the only ruling power from 1799 until 1867?" She stroked an imaginary beard.

"I wouldn't boast about having such an ancestor," Ivan sarcastically told her. "Baranof treated the Indians harshly and enslaved the Aleuts. Have you forgotten how the Tlingits revolted, massacred Russian citizens, and destroyed Sitka in 1802?" He lifted a sardonic eyebrow. "Or that Baranof was replaced fifteen years

101

later and the same Russian-American Company declined?"

"I have forgotten nothing," Nicolai retorted. He pointed to an open Bible on a nearby heavy table. "If Baranof and others had lived according to what is taught in those pages, how different Alaska might be today!" He sighed, brooding. "It is good that America rules." He shrugged and smiled at his daughter. "What will you name your new love?"

The question sponged away the shadow in her eyes. Like her father, Sasha believed in the power of love and justice. For hundreds of miles around, word of the Antons' integrity and devotion to the Indians ran like dogsleds on packed trails. "I don't know. Just Dog, for now. He needs a special name."

Dog yawned, showing pointed white teeth in an elfin smile. "You darling." Sasha hugged him again. One of her long braids tickled his nose. He sneezed a puppy sneeze and barked, then licked his new mistress's hand.

Ivan rose. "You might at least open my present." He handed her a small brown parcel.

A peculiar note in his voice alerted Sasha. *Oh, dear, why must he act so stiff and unyielding?* She longed for the good companion he had once been. Now a fierce look in his blue eyes she neither understood nor wanted to see there repelled her. *Why did everything have to change?* Strands of silver shone in her father's dark hair. She passionately wished she could turn back the hands of life's clock to a childhood of innocence and peace. Her sensitive lips quivered. If only Tarnigan could be as it once was. Nicolai Anton had stumbled on it years before, while still a young man. He found one of the few remaining Indian tribes that had somehow escaped desecration like so many other Alaskan tribes. He married and returned, vowing to spend the rest of his life keeping them so.

Lately, other white men had come to Tarnigan, bringing wives, children — and trouble. Nicolai and Sasha knew someone had begun sneaking whiskey to the Indian encampment. Unmistakable signs of it had surfaced.

"The curse of the white man can rage like wildfire through a tribe," Anton raved. "I've seen it happen."

"The world won't care." An unaccustomed gravity stilled the girl's mirth.

"They would if a work of art, a rare

painting, or cathedral were being destroyed," her father bitterly said. "Thousands of great men from all over the world would rise up, speak out, do something to stop the carnage. Why can't they do the same for a tribe created by God and headed for ruin? Why can't Washington see?" His heartbreak overflowed and he crashed his mighty fist to the table.

Sasha thought of the tribe. Her heart swelled. Few such Indians could be left in the world. Was there a lost tribe in the Amazon jungles that matched them? The Tarnigan Indians bore so little resemblance to those in southern Alaska it seemed they could not be of the same race. Bronzed and proud, the braves stood six feet or more, straight as fir trunks. The squaws were comely, the young girls exotic. From them Sasha had learned to wear her hair in braids in front of her shoulders. It pleased them and her.

"Are you going to open it or not?"

Ivan's impatient demand stopped her woolgathering. She undid the string, peeled back the brown paper, and hesitated. An oblong violet velvet jewel case lay in her hands. Dreading what was ahead, she touched a tiny spring. It opened. A string of fine pearls such as she had only seen in the stacks of magazines her father had sent to them shone in all its glory. Tiny diamonds in the clasp winked at her.

"Well?" Assurance oozed from the blond man. "Have you no thanks?"

She tore her gaze from the pearls and snapped the case shut. "I cannot accept it, Ivan."

He just stared at her and crossed his arms over his chest.

It seemed incredible such a fair face could darken so quickly. To Sasha, a glorious day had been overtaken by storm clouds. "I–I'm sorry," she stammered. "You must see, no girl can take such a present unless she is betrothed."

Ivan's smile returned. "That is all right with me. It's high time you promised to marry me. Isn't that right, Nicolai?" He turned toward his employer.

Nicolai's face showed mixed emotions. "I hardly think you have shown proper respect to either Anastasia or myself," he said shortly. "Have you been so long in the north you have forgotten a man speaks with the father privately before offering himself to the one he has chosen?"

Romanov's face flushed at the rebuke. "Surely you both know my intentions," he replied.

"Put the pearls away. I will speak with you later," Nicolai told him. Crestfallen, the would-be fiancé silently stuffed the jewel case into his flannel shirt and gave Sasha a hurt glance.

Her tender heart responded, as it always did. Yet this time she knew she must make clear her position. All the talking with Nicolai would not change her sisterly affection to the woman's love Ivan wanted from her. She took a deep breath.

"Please don't ask Father for my hand," she faltered. Inflicting pain was foreign to her healing nature, yet she sensed not to do so would bring further and deeper anguish. "You are the dearest friend I have, except for Naleenah. Can we not go on as we are? You will one day find a wife who loves you as I cannot."

Heedless of the frowning Nicolai, Ivan caught both her hands. "How do you know? I believe I can make you love me. There is no other suitable white man in Tarnigan, nay, in all of this part of Alaska." He had never been more attractive than in his ardent pursuit of what suddenly appeared to be unattainable, fighting for the girl he felt he must possess in order to carry out his dreams. "You've said yourself you love no other. Why not me? Marry me,

Sasha. I promise to make you happy."

"You would marry me knowing I don't love you?" She peered deep into his blue eyes.

He laughed confidently. "Love will come."

Troubled, she freed her hands. No woman could fail to feel swayed by such eloquence. Her mind raced. Perhaps Ivan had spoken truly. There was no other acceptable suitor anywhere near. The deep affection and comradeship they had shared might be enough. Could he carry out his promise to make her care — enough?

"No." The word burst into the hand-rubbed paneled pine room.

Ivan wheeled toward Nicolai, who had risen and stood staring at his employee as if he had never seen him before. "What did you say?"

"I said no." The trader stretched to his full six-foot height. So must his ancestors before him have magnificently faced their foes. "Little Flower must never marry a man unless she loves him with all her heart." The pronouncement rolled out like a death knell to Ivan's hopes. "There will be no learning to love after. She must come to you with the same adoration my beloved Jeanne brought to me."

Romanov's face blanched. His hands clenched and unclenched.

"Son, it is for your sake as much as hers," Nicolai sadly said. "Unless she loves in that way, you will be cheated of one of God's richest blessings. Her life will be one of sorrow and pain. No one, especially a woman, can pretend a love she does not feel, one that fills her with singing through tragedy and grief simply because her beloved is near. No man can fail to suspect the lack of that love. I have known them, men and women who felt love would come." His large head wagged from side to side.

"Shall I tell you what this love you so carelessly promise can be?" His dark eyes took on a faraway look. "I stood by the bedside as my Jeanne gave life to the child I created by the grace of God. My heart tore into two pieces when she smiled and whispered, 'I will see you in the morning.' I wanted to follow her in death.

"A small cry reminded me I could not. To do so would mean the giving of her life meant nothing, just as the giving of our Lord's life means nothing unless we accept it. I bathed my girl-child and looked into her face. Like a tiny white flower it was." Each word came through clenched teeth.

Naked agony showed in Nicolai's face.

"Jeanne had already chosen the name for the daughter she insisted she carried. Anastasia. She said it meant 'of the Resurrection, of springtime.' I declared she must also be Jeanne, 'God is gracious.' Had He not been gracious in leading me to the choicest woman in Alaska and blessing us with a child?" The thought brought a new wave of bitterness. "How could God take the wife of my youth? I pushed it aside and gazed at my daughter, both of our faces wetted by my tears. She wore her mother's face."

He stopped so long Sasha wondered if he would continue.

Nicolai drew in a long, quivering breath and let it go. "Never have I told another about that moment, until now. Little Flower became my springtime, my resurrection from despair, my hope and joy. She was a part of Jeanne left behind when she moved on, her final gift." He held out an upturned hand, as if pleading to be understood. "Ivan, I will not have you or any man rob Anastasia of what I have known." The next instant, he crossed the room and plunged out into the chilly evening.

Tears crowded Sasha's throat. She felt she had seen into the depths of her father's heart. His impassioned parting sentence burned in red-hot letters into her brain. "I will not have you or any man rob Anastasia of what I have known." Who could have suspected that beneath the rough exterior of Nicolai Anton lay such tender emotion? She felt shaken by the story she had never been told and would never again hear. Gone forever were the fancies Ivan's pleading had woven.

Dear God, she silently vowed. *I will be true. If You want me to marry, to experience what Father has had in his life, I know You will send someone. Until then, I will wait and never again consider marrying.*

Sasha fell from exaltation to the depths with Ivan's next words. "You don't have to listen to him." He seized her hands in a grip that hurt. "Nicolai has built your mother into some kind of woman who couldn't have existed and worships at her shrine. Why should it stop us from marrying? You're long past twenty-one. Come away with me. Tonight."

"You're hurting me." She tried to pull free.

His grip tightened. "Don't try to run away from me, Sasha. You're going to be my wife." Some of the cruelty and arrogance he had deplored in Alexander Baranof rose to the surface.

"Let me go!" She wrenched her hands free and rubbed at the red marks on her wrists. Her eyes blazed like Indian signal fires. Dog, which had stood watching the scene, growled low in his puppy throat and charged. Sasha scooped him into her arms. Spots redder than scarlet fever stood out on her white cheeks.

"You'd better leave, Ivan. If Father saw you treating me so, he'd beat you senseless and have you packed out of Tarnigan before you regained consciousness." The scorn in her voice lashed. "For the sake of our friendship, I don't intend to tell him — this time." She snuggled Dog closer.

Her icy stare brought him to his senses. He must not be sent away. A few more months and he'd be in a position to dictate terms to both of the Antons, his terms. "Sasha, forgive me," he cried. "There won't be another time. It's just that I love you so much I —"

She cut him off with a quick movement of her right hand. Dog, in the crook of her left arm, growled again and bared his teeth. "If I had ever considered I might learn to care, you just killed all chances."

"At least be my friend." A repentant look

111

chased the darkness from his face.

"I cannot promise that." She didn't give an inch. Deep in her heart she knew things could never be the same. She had seen in Ivan's eyes all lack of understanding when her father bared his very soul. His manner afterward had repelled and frightened her. Sasha walked to the door Nicolai had closed behind him.

Ivan silently stepped into the cold darkness after a final appealing glance, then cursed when the door shut and walked off toward his cabin adjoining the trading post.

The encounter left Sasha more shaken than she realized. Without lighting the oil lamps, she sank to a comfortable divan upholstered in tawny buckskin, her feet on a wolfskin rug. Dog whimpered and settled deep into her lap. She absently stroked him, reliving the birthday that had started so joyfully and ended in chaos. Gradually the snapping fire and peace of *Nika Illahee* stole into her aching heart.

She thought of the love between her father and mother and quieted. Did God have such a gift in store for her? A feeling she hadn't recognized in herself stirred. Until today she had been content to live with her father, racing behind a team of dogs and ahead of gathering storms.

"Like a child," she whispered. The same sadness that had enveloped her earlier returned, a melancholy longing to stop time even while the future beckoned with impatient fingers. What did it hold, those unplumbed days, months, and years ahead?

"What? Sitting in the dark?" Nicolai entered as soundlessly as a panther.

Glad for the normal note in his dear voice, Sasha stood so quickly Dog tumbled to the wolfskin rug with an indignant yip. "Sorry. I was thinking." She sensed her father's reluctance to discuss what had occurred and added, "How does dried apple pie sound for supper? After the venison roast, that is. I put apples to soak last night."

Her father smacked his lips. "Naleenah is bringing a cake." His hand flew to his mouth in chagrin. "I wasn't supposed to tell. She knew I'd chosen the pup and said she wanted to bring the cake. Don't let her know I said anything, will you? Go ahead and make the pies. I like them even better than her cake." His laugh rumbled in his massive chest. "Not only are you one of the best dog handlers in Tarnigan, you're also the best cook."

"Thanks to you." She laughed and

started toward the door leading to the cheerful kitchen with its windows on two sides and colorful tablecloth and chair covers. All the time she rolled out crusts, she marveled. How much she'd taken for granted! Her flour-covered hand rested on her big stirring spoon.

It couldn't have been easy for Father to be a mother as well. Sometimes he'd been forced to leave Sasha with a reliable Indian woman while he made his trips for supplies. Otherwise he had taken full care of her from the day of her birth. He'd held her chubby hands on the reins of the dog teams and laughed when she cried that she was driving. He had taught her to cook, using the same recipes her mother used before her. Most of all, Nicolai Anton had given her a knowledge of and faith in Jesus Christ.

"Jeanne cannot come back to us," he would say. "We must go to her one day when this life is over."

Once Sasha asked, "Will we take the dogsled?"

"No. God needs no sleds in heaven!" The laugh she loved bellowed out.

"Does Mama like it there? Is it beautiful, like Tarnigan?" she wanted to know.

"Yes, Little Flower." Nicolai took the big

Bible and turned pages. "The Apostle Paul says, 'But as it is written, Eye hath not seen, nor ear heard, neither have entered into the heart of man, the things which God hath prepared for them that love Him,' 1 Corinthians 2:9. That means we can't imagine what living in heaven will be like."

She found it hard to believe. "Lovelier than the colors of the aurora borealis? Or the sun shining on a glacier? Sweeter than the birds and singing spruce trees when the wind touches them?"

"Oh, yes." Certainty filled the big man's voice, and then humility.

"Remember, it's just for those who love Him."

"Did Mama love God?"

"More than life itself." His eyes glistened like raindrops. "So do I and so must you, Anastasia."

She never forgot their conversations. He talked with her as with other adults. He answered hundreds of childish questions. "How many stars are there? Why does Naleenah have browner skin than mine? Where does God live?"

The grown-up Sasha laughed and went back to her piemaking. Surely her father's wit and simple trust must have been sorely tried, yet she couldn't remember ever going to sleep dissatisfied, whether in bed, beneath the stars, or snuggling inside a tent while the elements raged. Sometimes Nicolai's best answers had been a simple, "We can't know that, child. We aren't God and only He has all the answers. Perhaps when we get to heaven we can ask Him. Or it may not matter then."

Sasha hummed, fitted the dough into her tins, and mixed the dried apples with cinnamon and sugar. Ivan liked pie almost as much as her father.

Her happiness fled at the familiar thought. In spite of what he had done, could she close the door on friendship, drive Ivan out into the cold, the way she'd done earlier?

"He had no right," she whispered rebelliously. Memory of something Nicolai had said long ago came to mind. Sasha had exploded when she learned someone might be furnishing whiskey to her Indian friends. "How can anyone be so terrible?" she demanded. "I'll never forgive whoever is doing it."

"Don't say that," her father warned. "You're the Christian and required to act like one, which means forgiving even when it's hard." Her father sighed. "The whiskey runners are not followers of Christ. We can't expect them to live like we are."

God said those who served Him must forgive. A tear dripped into her pie. *Why, oh why had Ivan spoiled things? Was he a Christian?* She realized she didn't know. He had always listened politely when she talked of her mother and heaven but never actually stated what, if anything, he believed about God.

Sasha finished her work in a subdued mood. Naleenah would come soon bearing a birthday cake and expecting to find the white girl she called sister ecstatic over her malamute birthday pup. Her keen dark eyes must not find anything amiss. Could Sasha pass muster and escape the younger girl's intuitive ability to spot trouble in her friend? She considered telling Naleenah what had happened. Although several years younger, the girls had been best friends since childhood, sharing dreams and secrets. When some of the young braves admiringly watched Naleenah, she only shrugged.

"Pooh! I'd rather be with you," she told Sasha.

Still, the troubled girl hesitated. *Was it right to tell?* Naleenah obviously enjoyed the teasing Ivan gave both girls when the three went on jaunts.

Sasha shook her head. Better to say nothing. Why, then, did the thought of holding something back from Naleenah leave her restless and uneasy?

Chapter 7

Of all the Indian maidens in Tarnigan, Naleenah, daughter of Tonglaw, possessed the most charm and grace. Sapling straight, she appeared taller than her five feet, six inches, Sasha's height. Her glossy black braids and slim but rounded body also resembled her friend's. The keenest northern-trained eyes often had trouble telling the parka-clad girls apart at a distance when they ran behind a dogsled.

Both white-skinned Sasha and Naleenah, whose rich brown skin set off white teeth and laughing dark eyes, reflected superb physical development and the simple joy of living.

"Plenty of fresh air, sunshine, and good food," Nicolai liked to say. "Why shouldn't they be as they are? Is this not God's own country, unsmirched by city soot and grime? What a pair!"

The village agreed. Yet seasoned traders

and *cheechaquos* (newcomers, tenderfeet) alike found it significant that admiration for the girls' beauty ran second to respect for their prowess with rifle, pistol, and sled. It took skill to survive in the diverse land where grandeur so often changed to tragedy in the twinkling of a star. First one girl, then the other won the impromptu races they staged for their own enjoyment or participated in on holidays. Other maidens ran with them, but for the past few years, none had proved fleet of foot enough to claim the honors the friends shared.

"Sasha has a little extra stamina because of being older," Nicolai told onlookers at every Tarnigan race. "But Naleenah runs like a startled deer." His hearty laugh bellowed. "Thinking one is better is like saying the rainbow is more beautiful than the sunrise. Did not God create them all?"

No thought of races or competitions detracted from the girls' enjoyment of Sasha's birthday. A slight tap on the kitchen door announced Naleenah's presence, and Sasha ran to throw it wide.

"Why, Naleenah." Her eyes widened with pretended surprise. "What a beautiful cake!" She reached to touch the swirls of white frosting with an inquiring forefinger, but the Indian girl smiled and stepped back.

"Your father must see it before you spoil it with your finger," she scolded. A lilt in her voice and her upturned mouth brought a matching smile to Sasha's. In her pale buckskin shirt and short skirt, she looked even younger than she really was.

Naleenah's innocent, "Where is Ivan? I thought he'd be here," erased Sasha's smile.

She turned to stir the kettle of stew and give herself time to adjust her expression. "He had to go." She desperately fought to sound normal and peeked into the oven at the nicely browning dried apple pies.

"On your birthday?" The other girl sounded incredulous. She set the cake on the table.

Sasha decided to change the subject. "How do you like my present?" She whirled away from the stove and pointed.

The malamute pup had finally tired of following Sasha around while she made pies. Just before Naleenah arrived, Dog had unerringly chosen the warmest spot next to the big black stove and subsided into a tired ball. Now he slept, plumy tail curved around him. His nose lay tucked under his front paws that one day would

skim the frozen snow as his ancestors before him.

"He's pick of the litter." Fondness crept
into Naleenah's dark eyes.

"I know. He's going to be the best sled
dog in Alaska," Sasha bragged. She gave a
secret sigh of relief. So far she'd not betrayed how upset Ivan had made her.

"He could be," Naleenah agreed. "Have
you named him?"

"Not yet. Do you have any ideas?" Sasha
hopefully asked. The longer she could
sidetrack her friend, the better.

Dark brows knitted. Naleenah stared at
the puppy. "Name him Kobuk, after the
river." She giggled and her whole face
lighted. "It's strong, wayward, and
curving." She lightly touched the circle of
fur. "So is he!"

Sasha laughed out loud. "Kobuk he will
be."

The pup opened one clear blue eye,
yipped, yawned, and went back to sleep.

"He must like his name. Did you notice?
His eyes are as blue as Ivan's."

"Don't ever tell Ivan that!" Sasha made a
face. "I did earlier. He was *not* pleased."

"So that's why he isn't here." Naleenah
looked wise.

"Not really. We had a–an argument

about his birthday gift to me." The memory brought a rush of indignation. "My word, he brought me a string of pearls fit for the Queen of Sheba. As if I could accept such a present!"

Her friend sat curiously still.

Heedless of anything but remembered anger, Sasha went on. "He should have known better. Those pearls would feed everyone in Tarnigan for months, maybe years. It's not as if we were betrothed. Even if we were, what use have I for such baubles?"

"You would wear them if Ivan took you to the great cities he has told us about," Naleenah reminded.

She sounded so sad Sasha cried out, "Leave Tarnigan and you and Father? Never!"

The shadow did not leave the dusky, watching face. "A woman must follow her man, even if the trails are long and hard."

"Ivan isn't my man." Sasha broke off before she repeated his pleas to be just that. "He never will be." Conviction steadied her voice. No matter what happened, she could not, would not, marry the man she loved as a brother. Not after Father's story and her own vow. Again she considered telling her sisterlike friend the whole tale but refrained.

Naleenah's high spirits returned. "I am glad." Her eyes glistened like shiny pieces of black lava. "I would be lonely."

Sasha cocked her head to one side. "A number of braves would like to change that," she teased.

"Pah." Naleenah dismissed them with a wave of her shapely hand. "I love none of them, with their boasting. They stand and watch me, so." She crossed her arms in front of her chest, tucked in her chin, and looked haughty.

Sasha rocked with laughter. "If we lived elsewhere, you could become a great actress." Laughter pealed again. "You look exactly like the braves. What does Tonglaw say?"

Naleenah's arms dropped to her sides. "He says I must choose someday. However, he is not eager to give his only child away, even for fine beaver or marten skins. Not even for silver fox."

Sasha thought of the few silver fox pelts she had seen, rippling like tossing waves under the full moon's glow. Their rarity made them precious, desirable above the great bales of glossy mink, silken ermine, and fiery red fox that lay in abundance in Nicolai Anton's fur cache. The Indians trapped and traded them for supplies.

Anton, in turn, used them to barter for the wide variety of goods he kept in the trading post Ivan Romanov managed. A stone and turf storage room stood behind the Anton house, half underground to protect the furs against heat and cold. A huge padlock on the heavy door guarded the prime pelts from those willing to sell their soul and chance of heaven for the wealth stacked to the ceiling of the domed room.

"If only the Indians lived in Tarnigan, I'd never need the lock," Nicolai had said at breakfast just a few days earlier. "They have no need to steal. What they want they can trap." A frown marred his usual genial countenance.

"What is it, Father?"

He told her with obvious reluctance, "I've seen footprints near the door and scratches on the lock."

Sasha's fork clattered to her plate. "You mean someone in Tarnigan is trying to rob us?" Her voice rose to a high pitch. "How can he? Everyone here knows the law of the cache. He who steals is no better than a murderer, for he takes the owner's protection against hunger and winter. Not in our case, of course, but it's still transgressing the law."

"I know and it saddens me. Little Flower, how I wish Tarnigan could have remained as it once was. It is not so. Even here, away from civilization, we are not safe from the horde of those filled with lust and greed."

"Yes." She sighed. Shortly after the stampede to the Yukon in search of gold in the Klondike began the previous autumn, first one, then another bearded man whose faces showed havoc from mysterious pasts drifted into the village. Gossip had it they fled from killings in the gold fields. Some moved on. Others did not. The Antons found it menacing that the first sign of whiskey among the Indians showed at about the same time. So far they had been unable to discover the source.

"Sasha, you have left me in spirit."

Naleenah's quiet reminder returned her to the present. "Why must men fight and rob and do terrible things?" she demanded.

Used to her friend's quick mental leaps from subject to subject, Naleenah just shook her head. "Tomorrow is enough time to think on such unpleasantness. Today is a time to celebrate your day of birth. Call your father and I will cut the cake." She hesitated and a soft look stole into her eyes. "Can you not forgive Ivan enough to invite him to return?"

Sasha squirmed. Her friend's suggestion came so close to her own earlier thoughts it surprised her. Ostracizing Ivan without all of Tarnigan knowing was impossible. Neither could she get away with it unless she told her father. She must not. She had only seen him in a towering rage a few times, but it left her frightened. Once he banished a village inhabitant after he caught the drunken man unmercifully beating the sled dogs he'd driven to the point of exhaustion. Sasha shivered. The tongue-lashing the man received matched what he'd done to the tired team. So would Ivan fare if Father ever found out how rude and threatening his trading post manager had been to his beloved daughter.

"Run and ask him to come," she impulsively told Naleenah. The next instant two strong arms encircled her and the Indian girl left a soft kiss on Sasha's cheek before she glided out the door.

"Well, I never." Sasha gazed at the door in astonishment. "Who'd have dreamed she'd care that much whether Ivan came or not, even if it is my birthday?" Her face cleared. "Oh, of course. She hates discord. Isn't she always settling quarrels in the tribe? She can't bear for Ivan and me to be at odds."

Ten minutes later they returned. Unaccustomed red spots shone in Naleenah's smooth cheeks and made her prettier than ever. Ivan eyed Sasha uncertainly, then shook himself as a husky shakes off snow. "Thanks for asking me."

"Thanks for coming." She forced herself to match his lightness, even when something deep in his eyes flickered.

His voice roused the malamute. The pup uncurled in one fluid movement, bared his teeth, snarled, then hurled himself at Romanov.

"Kobuk, stop that!" For the second time Sasha scooped her dog into her arms. He struggled to get down and yipped.

"Noisy little beast." Yet Sasha saw admiration in Ivan's face. She knew he respected a fighter. She opened her mouth to speak, but he forestalled her. "Why did you decide on that name?"

"Naleenah says he's like the river: strong, wayward, and curving."

Ivan had the grace to laugh. "Well, he's wayward and curving and someday he will be strong. In the meantime, let's see if we can change his mind about me." He glanced around the kitchen, then strode to the stove, selected a small piece of meat from the stew, and blew on it. When cooled, he placed it in the palm of his hand and slowly walked toward Sasha and the still-growling pup. "Here, Kobuk."

The pup's nostrils quivered at the rich meaty smell, but he made no move to accept the peace offering. Undaunted, Ivan held it closer, then snatched his hand back. He glared at Kobuk, who wriggled and barked at the top of his puppy lungs.

"By the great horn spoon, what's carrying on in here?" Nicolai appeared in the doorway leading to the living room.

"The cur snapped at me." Ivan's face darkened with anger. "What kind of dog's he going to make, barking his fool head off and trying to bite anyone who comes near him?"

"Must just be notional. He didn't act that way toward me. Naleenah?" She shook her head.

"Actually, I'm glad he doesn't cozy up to a whole lot of people," Nicolai slowly said. "The day's coming when Sasha's safety could well lie in the fact her dog distrusts strangers."

"He should be able to tell the difference between friend and foe," Ivan retorted.

A look of suspicion crossed Anton's face. "Yes, he should."

129

Sasha held her breath. Surely Father couldn't suspect —

"The river for which the little one is named goes its own winding way," Naleenah, the peacemaker, said. "So will Kobuk."

"Kobuk? Now, that's a grand name." Nicolai's massive hand rested on the gray and white head for a moment and the pup stilled. "Anastasia, is this a birthday party or a funeral? I'm ready for a piece of Naleenah's cake, even if you aren't. After the stew, of course," he hastily added. He stepped into the living room, brought back a large flat Indian basket, and lined it with a soft towel Sasha handed him. "Come on, Kobuk. You can stay inside for a few days, then it's outdoors for you. No soft dogs around here." He set the basket, protesting pup and all, inside the living room and closed the door firmly. A few scrabbles and yips followed, then silence.

"As long as we don't hear anything we'll know he isn't tearing up the place," Nicolai observed dryly. "Sit down, everyone. I'm starving."

The kettle of stew and most of the cake vanished before appetites made large by hard work. Nicolai longingly eyed the warm apple pies set to cool, but Sasha shook her head. "Another piece of cake, Father?"

"Of course." He smiled at Naleenah. "Someone's going to get a good cook as well as a good wife."

Sasha noticed lovely color rise to her friend's face before the Indian girl smiled a bit shyly. She glanced at Ivan. He also sat looking at Naleenah, an unreadable look in his eyes. It remained such a short time, she wondered if it were her imagination. She served more cake to her father, glad her birthday hadn't been spoiled after all. She felt even more so when Ivan helped Naleenah dry dishes after Sasha washed them, as he had a hundred or more times before. Everything felt normal again. If only it could remain so!

With her guests' departure, some of her happiness went with the laughing couple. Sasha wandered into the living room, received Kobuk's joyful greetings, and sat down on the buckskin-upholstered divan with the pup in her lap. Firelight and glimmering lamplight restored some of her peace.

"I wonder what we'll be doing a year from now," she mused aloud.

Nicolai looked up from a journal he'd been reading, his dark gaze quizzical. "Why so pensive, Little Flower?"

Unwilling to share the real reason, she mumbled, "I suppose the passing of each year makes you wonder. Father, thank you for what you said today." She didn't wait for him to answer. The moment was too fragile and precious. "I think I'll go to bed, if you don't mind. It's been quite a day." Her lips trembled.

He opened his great arms to her and tenderly kissed her white forehead. "Good night, child. May the great God bless you richly." Like a benediction, it rolled over her troubled heart. She slept, untouched by the future.

Long before her twenty-third year had passed, change came to Tarnigan, the Antons, Naleenah, and Ivan. Winter arrived early and with it more news of the gold rush. A town named Dawson sprang up to house the miners, city dwellers, and hangers-on who flooded the area surrounding Bonanza Creek. Thousands came for gold. Few found it. By the time most of the genuine and would-be prospectors arrived, all the good claims had been staked out. Still they came, willing to risk their lives and face avalanches, hardship, and death. Poorly equipped in many cases, they stumbled into Dawson disillusioned and broke. The Yukon became a territory. Dawson, home to about twenty-five thousand of the estimated thirty-five thousand in Yukon Territory at the height of the rush, was named the capital.

Over seven thousand boats passed down the Yukon River in 1898, carrying twenty-eight thousand people. A good five thousand, many of them lawless, came by other routes. The Northwest Mounted Police patrolled the region to maintain some semblance of order. Yet debauchery and killings did not cease.

As Nicolai predicted, hunted men turned their faces north and west, determined to escape their relentless pursuers by losing themselves in the harsh country beyond the sound of miners' cries for revenge. Many lost their lives. Others joined forces with those as unsavory as themselves, men with haunted pasts.

January 1899 passed quietly enough in Tarnigan. February brought extreme cold and blizzards. One late February night Sasha and her father sat in front of a blazing fire that defied falling thermometers and a snow-clad world to destroy its cheer and warmth. Ivan had dropped in earlier, then excused himself, saying he had work to do.

" 'Tis a hard taskmaster you have, requiring that you work so hard." Nicolai looked at him sternly, although a twinkle shone in his dark eyes.

Ivan shrugged into his fur-lined parka. "Tonglaw brought in some pelts and I didn't have time to tally them," he explained. "I'll see you both tomorrow. Brrr. Wish spring would come, but the way it's going, I expect it will be late this year."

Sasha caught the wistful glance he sent her and smiled back, but not with her old freedom. Sometimes she wished she could lay aside forever his hateful behavior of so many months ago. Yet each time she grew friendly, the spark she feared and distrusted lurked in his blue eyes.

After he had gone, she sat brooding. Outwardly, nothing had changed between them. Ivan, Sasha, Naleenah, and Nicolai sped over the packed snows as they had done for years, laughing and calling, giving the growing Kobuk as much training as was good for him. Close to a year old, he little resembled the feisty pup that once cuddled in his mistress's lap, although if permitted, he'd leap on her in a frenzy of canine adoration whenever she appeared. He also warned off other dogs that might come too close to the girl who owned him, body, mind, and heart.

Inwardly, everything had changed. Enlightened by her glimpse into unsuspected, hidden depths, Sasha worked hard to ensure she and Ivan were never alone. When he invited her on an outing, she always responded, "Of course. We'll be glad to come." She clung to Naleenah, using her as a buffer with which to keep the peace without being manipulated into an uncomfortable scene.

This particular evening she involuntarily sighed. Her dark hair, down for once, foamed around her white, flannel-clad shoulders. Something, woman's intuition, perhaps, told her Ivan would not always allow things to go on in this way. *If only she had someone to turn to!* She glanced at her father, debated, and shook her head. She could not ask his advice without betraying the long-held secret of the birthday confrontation. He would demand to know why she had not spoken at the time or in the long months since.

Naleenah? Sasha forgot her worries and thought of her friend. Where had her companion gone? The girl was so filled with gaiety she resembled a flitting butterfly in a field of brilliant flowers. But the early winter had taken a toll. Naleenah looked

135

thin and worn. Seldom did her bright smile flash and sadness rested in her eyes like a bird on its nest. Several times Sasha had inquired, asking if the other girl felt well. Naleenah always put aside what troubled her and chatted feverishly.

Perhaps Father knew. Sasha started to ask, then observed new silver streaks in his hair and the deepened lines in his face. Scarcely a week passed without new evidence coming forth of whiskey touching the lives of the Indian village. In addition, the padlock on the fur cache had been secretly smashed one blizzardy night and thousands of dollars of rich pelts stolen. The storm hid both the breaking of the lock and all traces of the thieves. No, she could not bother him with Naleenah's secret troubles when he had so many of his own.

Frantic pounding on the heavy door interrupted Sasha's reverie. The door flung open. A fur-clad, snow-whitened figure staggered in, along with a blast of wintry air that set the fireplace flames dancing and all but blew out the oil lamps.

"What on earth —" Nicolai and Sasha sprang up at the same time. He raced to the door and closed out the screeching night.

Snow-covered wraps fell to the floor. A shaking brown hand reached out to Sasha and the visitor took a step toward her.

"Naleenah! For mercy's sake, what are you doing out on a night like this?"

In all their years of friendship, Sasha had never seen the girl so distraught. The dark eyes looked glazed. No hint of color touched the curiously blanched cheeks.

"I had no choice." Her gaze darted around the room.

Sasha felt Naleenah saw little. "Come to the fire."

"Don't let them get me." A broken little cry came from Naleenah's pale lips.

Nicolai strode to the girls. He took Naleenah's hands and rubbed them. "Child, you are safe here. You know that." He scowled when Sasha started to speak. "Not now. Bring coffee, as hot as she can take it." He led the younger girl closer to the fireplace and gently pushed her into a chair. With strong hands made gentle by tending hurt creatures, man and beast alike, he removed her soaked moccasins.

She stretched her feet toward the fire with a little sound and opened her mouth.

"Don't try to talk until you drink your coffee," Nicolai ordered.

Sasha could hardly bear the wounded

expression on her friend's face. Who was she afraid of, to leave home in the middle of a blizzard looking for help?

Naleenah drained the cup. Her hands steadied.

"All right, child. What is it? Why aren't you home where you belong?"

Fear returned to her face. "I cannot go home. Ever." Desolation stamped itself on her face, making her look older than the Endicott Mountains.

"Why, Naleenah?" Nicolai knelt beside her chair.

"Men promised Father whiskey, if he . . . if I . . . I will die before I let them touch me!"

"Dear God," Nicolai breathed, not a curse, but a prayer that went into Sasha's heart and echoed. "Surely Tonglaw didn't agree!" He leaped to his feet and looked down at the girl who bowed her head in shame and shrank beneath his glare.

One tear trickled from beneath a lowered eyelid. Then Naleenah said in a voice that tore Sasha's heart to ribbons, "Yes."

Chapter 8

Sasha's knees gave way. She felt the same way the time ice broke on a small lake she thought would never crack. She'd plunged into freezing, black depths. Only her father's quick actions saved her from drowning or coming down with pneumonia. Now she dropped to the wolfskin rug and swallowed hard to keep nausea from overcoming her. Never had she faced anything so slimy and evil as what the storm had brought into her home. The sin abroad in this horrible February night left her feeling sickened, as dirty and tainted as if she were the one betrayed.

Naleenah sat with her head bowed. So had Sasha seen generations of mourning Indian women sit. *Please, God, help me know what to say to her,* Sasha silently prayed. She made her way to her friend.

"Don't look like that, Naleenah," she fiercely said. "It is not your fault. You are good and clean and wonderful."

Anguished dark eyes looked up. "But my father . . ." Naleenah could not finish her sentence.

"Tonglaw is only partly to blame for this wickedness. It is more the fault of the accursed men who have brought destruction to the Indians of Tarnigan." Nicolai's voice rolled out like a prophet of old, pronouncing judgment on the unrepentant inhabitants of a far-distant land. "Once Tonglaw and his braves first tasted whiskey, it set a raging fire inside them, a desire for more. It lighted an even stronger one in their minds. Oh, my people, my people." Unashamed tears coursed down his rugged cheeks and he suddenly looked old.

"Father, we must find those who are responsible and punish them!" Sasha rose and pounded her fist on the arm of the divan where the weeping Naleenah huddled into a ball of misery.

"We will. They will be driven away, even if it is the dead of winter," he promised.

A pounding at the door sent Naleenah into Nicolai's arms with a shriek. "Don't let them take me!"

"No one will take you." The big trader released her, but Sasha clasped Naleenah tightly. Nicolai set his jaw in a hard line, crossed the room in three mighty strides, and yanked open the door. For the second time that evening a snowy, furred figure fell into the room, along with another blast of subzero, flake-laden air. Nicolai threw his great shoulder against the door to shut out the howling storm. Great chunks of snow fell to the floor from the newcomer's clothing.

"Ivan?" Nicolai gasped.

Ivan? How could he be so snowy just running the short distance between the trading post where he'd gone to work and their home, Sasha wondered. She forgot her concerns when Ivan threw back the hood of his parka and she caught sight of his face, bloodless and ghastly in the firelight.

"Naleenah? Are you all right?" Romanov demanded hoarsely. He stared at the Indian girl as if seeing a specter.

She didn't answer.

"Naleenah!" Ivan's face twisted. "I — you — *what have they done to you?*" He stumbled toward the girl who stood in the protective circle of Sasha's arms as if she'd been turned to stone.

"Some rotter has filled Tonglaw with whiskey," Nicolai announced. "He promised Naleenah, in return for the firewater to warm his belly and quench the kindled flames."

"You escaped in time?" Dull red suffused Ivan's fair face. A suggestion of foam came to the lips he licked as if they had suddenly gone dry.

"Yes, and she is never going back. Never!" Sasha cried. "How can men be so wicked?" Her voice rang loud in the cozy room. "Oh, but I hope they are caught. They should be whipped before all of the village."

Ivan turned ashen. His gaze never left the trembling Indian girl, who sagged against her girlish defender. "Thank God you are safe."

"Little Flower, take her to your room, get her dried and into warm clothes," Nicolai ordered.

With another glance at Ivan, who still stared at Naleenah, Sasha obeyed. Yet all the time she helped her friend, she rebelled. Her father had taught her from childhood how God brought good from everything. She silently shook her head in protest. No good could come from this night's evil deeds. She led Naleenah to the small bench in front of her dressing table and briskly toweled the long, dark hair before brushing it to its usual satin smoothness. "We won't braid it yet," she told the drooping girl. "You can sit in front of the fireplace and it won't take long to dry."

"Sasha? Did you mean it, about my not going back?"

She looked straight into the shadowed dark eyes reflected in the mirror. Even the light from a nearby lamp couldn't hide the dullness so unlike Naleenah's usual sparkling gaze.

"With all my heart."

"Then you don't hate me because of what Father did?"

"Hate you! I could as soon hate part of myself." The brush clattered to the floor and Sasha shook her friend even while tears shone through her laughter. "Aren't we as close as sisters? We always will be, Naleenah."

"I pray it will be so."

Sasha barely caught the low words. "It will be. Tomorrow Father will go to Tonglaw." She felt a shudder go through the younger girl's shoulders.

"I wanted to tell you, but I could not."

Sasha stared at the drawn, mirrored reflection. "You mean, all these weeks, this is what has been bothering you?" Incredulity filled her and her grip on Naleenah tightened.

"Yes, but I never thought Father would do it. When Silvertip g–gave his squaw to a white man for a bottle of whiskey, I was too ashamed to tell. Besides, Father threatened to banish me from the tribe." Her muffled voice sent chills through Sasha. "Before the whiskey came, we were happy. Father had begun to listen to the stories of Jesus you taught me. Now he is drunken and cares nothing except for the drink that makes him crazy." She drew in a sobbing breath. "If I had not overheard what the men said when they came tonight, I —"

"Don't, Naleenah!" Sasha couldn't stand the pain in the low voice. "You are here and safe." She gradually comforted the shaking girl until she grew calm enough to go back to the living room.

Ivan and Nicolai rose when the girls entered. Some of the color had come back to the manager's face, but he clenched and unclenched his hands. "Tonglaw must pay for this."

"The man or men behind it are the ones to uncover and punish." Nicolai had regained some of his composure. "Why haven't I seen? I blame myself for that." Shame tinged his face. "I knew some of the braves drank when they could get hold of whiskey, but this!" He spread his hands.

"Naleenah, just how far have things gone, anyway?" He seated himself and bent a piercing look toward her.

She cast a despairing glance at Sasha, then looked down. Sasha led her to a chair. Her beautiful shining hair fell about her like a curtain. Sasha knelt on the wolfskin rug and patted her friend's hand. Anger overcame her reluctance to bring up a subject she would normally never discuss even with Naleenah, let alone her father or Ivan. In a hard, tight voice she said, "This isn't the first incident. Silvertip sold his squaw for whiskey."

Nicolai leaped to his feet like a tawny lynx to its prey. "What!" His roar matched the still-growing wind raging above their heads and down the chimney. "Is this true?"

Tragedy of the ages rested in Naleenah's beautiful face when she flung back her hair and said quietly, "It is true."

"Why didn't you tell me?" Nicolai cried. "How could you keep silent about such a monstrous thing?"

The curtain of hair swung back again, hiding the girl's convulsed face.

"She was ashamed, Father, ashamed of Silvertip and her tribe," Sasha explained.

"So it has come, the thing we feared and

dreaded. God have mercy on Tarnigan. Our peace and happiness are at an end." Nicolai's face turned gray and he collapsed into his chair. He stared into the fire, then said in a heavy voice, "Well, there's one who won't be an innocent victim, a sacrifice to this madness. Naleenah, from this moment on, you are my beloved daughter and Sasha's sister. You will remain with us until you marry. If you choose not to do so, you are welcome to live in my home as long as you — or I — live." He didn't wait for an answer but turned to other things.

"There is no use going to the Indian encampment this night. The harm has been done. Tomorrow I will see Tonglaw."

"Perhaps he won't let you adopt Naleenah."

"Ivan!" Sasha's sharp protest brought color to his face, but Nicolai held up his massive hand. He threw his head back in the gesture that had earned him the title "White Father."

"He will, even if I have to buy her from him."

Sasha drew in a quick, hurting breath. Her chest felt constricted. "If you buy her, Tonglaw will have money for whiskey."

"It is the lesser of two evils," her father said brokenly. "We must protect Naleenah at all costs. Then, I intend to scour Tarnigan, nay, all of Alaska if necessary, and drive out those who inflame men with drink until they lay aside all honor. Sasha, put Naleenah to bed. I want to talk with Ivan."

Long after the exhausted Indian girl slept, cuddled up to Sasha for security, the white girl lay wide-eyed, staring into the darkness. Outside, the storm continued, but no stronger than the storm in Sasha's soul. Her whole way of life had been threatened.

Dear God, she silently prayed, *how could You let such a thing happen? It isn't God's fault,* a little voice whispered deep in her soul. *He gave those He created the right to choose good or evil.* Again she wondered: How could anything good come out of this turmoil? Hadn't Ivan cried out gratefulness to God for Naleenah's safety, something she had never heard him do in all their years of friendship? Perhaps this tragic time would turn her father's manager to God as nothing else could do. His voice had rung like a deep-toned church bell when he thanked God.

What would it do to Naleenah's faith? Hour after hour Sasha lay rigid, unwilling to disturb the stuporlike sleep into which the other girl had fallen. Could she continue to accept the white man's God after being so cruelly hurt by those who scoffed and broke His laws? The winter storm passed by, leaving downed trees and broken branches to be cleared away on the morrow. The human wreckage caused by greed and lust could not be disposed of so easily.

Nicolai Anton came home from his interview with Tonglaw wearing a set smile that fooled no one. All Sasha could get out of him was that he had been successful in his quest.

"I am taking no chances," he said shortly. "Ivan is preparing a contract. Although Tonglaw is ashamed and agrees this is best for Naleenah now, I want no repercussions later." He refused to say more or to tell what price he had given for the Indian girl.

"It's hard to believe people can still be bought and sold in a place belonging to the United States of America," Sasha marveled. "I guess Lincoln's freeing of the slaves doesn't count up here."

"Sadly, that is true." Nicolai inhaled, then blew out a mighty breath. "Say nothing to Naleenah except that I have arranged things." He forced a smile. "Now, let's see about turning that storeroom next to your bedroom into a place for her. There will be times when you will both need privacy. The rooms have a connecting door as well as the doors into the hall."

Diverted by the amount of work ahead, Sasha ran to tell her friend the news. They donned working clothes and started their tasks; by nightfall Naleenah had a room of her own. A search of the village unearthed a battered bed and dresser not being used. Nicolai promised to restore it when he could. From the trading post came warm blankets, and the Antons' private stock of pillows, towels, and other items furnished the rest. Nicolai wouldn't allow Naleenah to go home even to get her clothing, but grimly marched out, armed with his contract and whatever sum he and Tonglaw had agreed on for a purchase price. He privately told Sasha he intended to formally adopt Naleenah as soon as he could get the right papers recorded.

Although Sasha loved her friend, she secretly felt glad they'd have separate rooms. With girlhood behind and womanhood ahead, the desire for privacy Nicolai mentioned was real and important.

Yet Sasha rejoiced in Naleenah's presence. Before February ended, she found it hard to remember a time when the Indian girl had not been with the Antons. She never intruded but became a vital element in their family. Her quick hands relieved Sasha of many household tasks and her returning gaiety brightened the long winter days in the far northern world.

"I can't wait for spring," Sasha disconsolately said one March afternoon. "For some reason, it feels like winter has gone on forever." She pressed her nose to the glass of the living room window, which reflected flames from the fireplace.

Naleenah looked up from a stocking she'd been mending. Her long fingers lay idle for a moment. "I will be glad for spring, too."

Sasha turned, glad to see the tense look in the smooth face had given way to contentment. Peace rested in the dark eyes. "How about a run with the dogs? I'm so restless I can't stay inside. Every time I visit Kobuk, he looks at me so reproachfully it makes me feel guilty."

Doubt crept into Naleenah's face. "I don't know. Your father predicted another storm and he's almost always right."

"Almost," Sasha reminded. "Do come. We won't be gone for long."

Naleenah sighed and laid the stocking aside. "All right, but we must tell Nicolai."

"We can't." Sasha started toward her bedroom to change into warm clothing.

"He told me he was going to check on a family the other side of the village. By the time we hunt him up, it will be too late. I'll leave a note."

Naleenah stood stock-still. Consternation swept over her face. "Maybe we shouldn't go, Sasha."

"Mercy, what can happen to us in an hour? That's about all the daylight we have left." She looked out the window again. "Hurry and get ready."

Naleenah sighed again, but once outdoors, racing behind the sled, banners of color waved in her face and her laugh rang out.

"Look at Kobuk!"

With his first year behind him, the malamute already showed traces of the champion both girls felt he would become. Perfectly marked, strong of bone and sinew, his furry tail curled over his back in a great plume. His blue eyes reflected summer skies at their bluest and his powerful chest and legs set him apart even at this age as a magnificent lead dog in practice runs. Young and strong, he led the other four, keeping them in line as he'd done since the first time he led.

Over the snowy trail worn down by other men and dogs they flew, past blue-green spruces hung heavy with burdens of white. So great was the thrill of the run, they failed to note how far they had come from Tarnigan until a great, dark cloud obliterated most of the remaining daylight.

"Sasha, we have to turn back," Naleenah called, automatically slowing her pace. Sasha glanced over her shoulder, laughing and still running at full speed. "So soon?" In that split second she failed to notice the danger ahead. Neither did Kobuk nor his companions. A great chunk of trail had broken away, leaving a deep hole cunningly disguised by a layer of ice. The next instant the team broke through. The sled fell in on top of the howling dogs.

Slightly off balance, Sasha's momentum carried her forward. She caught her foot on a runner, eliciting a sharp pain in her leg, and staggered, just enough to send her tumbling into the wreckage of dogs and sled.

"Naleenah!"

"Sasha!" The Indian girl raced forward. Strong hands untangled her friend from the squirming mass of dogs and pulled her from the hole. "Are you hurt?"

"My leg." Sasha struggled to her feet, ripped off a furlined glove, and pressed her hand against her leggings. A warm wetness alerted her. "It's bleeding, but it can't be that bad. Good thing my leggings are thick. My word, are the dogs killed?"

"I hope not." Naleenah jerked the twisted sled free, grasped the collar of the nearest dog, and hauled him out. She did the same for three more.

"Kobuk?" She peered into the gloomy pit. "Oh, no!" A furry body lay motionless at the bottom.

"What's wrong?" Panic erased Sasha's faintness from the pain in her torn leg.

"It's Kobuk. He isn't moving."

Sasha flung herself down at the edge of the hole.

"Hang onto my feet," she ordered. A flare of pain reminded her. "No, I'll hold yours." She grasped Naleenah's ankles with hands made iron-strong by fear. "Can you get him?"

"Y–yes." But it took all Naleenah's superb strength to gather the inert dog in her arms and lift him out. She rolled back from the edge of the treacherous hole and lay panting until she could get her breath. "Is he — ?"

Exploring fingers told Sasha what she

153

needed to know. "He isn't dead, but I feel blood. A lot of it. He went in head-first." She took him into her lap, unwound the heavy scarf from her neck, and bound it around Kobuk's bleeding head.

"Head wounds always bleed a lot," Naleenah said and added, "I felt sharp rocks when I worked getting the dogs out."

"You have to go for help." Sasha strained her eyes to see in the growing murk. "I can't walk fast enough on this leg and the sled's broken. Can you make it? It's practically dark."

"Of course." Naleenah didn't waste time arguing. "The other dogs are nervous but unhurt. Poor Kobuk got the worst of it." With the last of the daylight, she straightened the dogs' harness and turned them toward Tarnigan. "I won't be too long. Mush," she called and vanished into the encroaching night. The sound of the dogs gradually dwindled, then died.

A low whimper came from the limp bundle of fur in Sasha's arms. A convulsive shudder went through Kobuk's frame as a wave of thankfulness washed over Sasha. "You're going to be fine," she crooned and hugged him. "Naleenah will be back with Father and he's as good as a doctor. He will take care of you."

Something wet and soft splatted against her bare hand. She hastily pulled on her glove. The next one hit her nose. "Looks like that black cloud meant business," she told her dog. If these flakes heralded a blizzard, she and the wounded Kobuk needed shelter. Northern-trained, she considered and rejected ideas. No sense wasting time trying to make a snow cave. Naleenah would be back before she did more than tire herself. Alternatives flashed through her mind. She closed her eyes and used all the intelligence bestowed on her by God and developed by her father. A picture of the terrain they'd been traveling flashed into her mind. She focused on the spruce trees they had passed. Not as good as fir, but they would do. If she could hobble to them and crawl beneath the branches, she and Kobuk would have shelter.

What if something happens and Naleenah doesn't come? The horrid thought chilled her.

"Come on, Kobuk. We have to move. Besides," she defiantly told the ever-nearing storm. "If worst comes to worst, we'll set a tree on fire and keep warm." Thank God for Nicolai having drilled survival skills into her since childhood! Always carry a knife, keep matches in a waterproof case, pack a chocolate bar for extra energy.

"We live in a land whose summer smile hides winter treachery," he'd warned. "Never leave the village without those three items. To do so is to let nature get the upper hand. More experienced men than I have lost their lives by a moment of carelessness."

She grimaced. A moment of carelessness had resulted in her being hurt. She removed her glove again and found that although her leg throbbed and burned like fire, no more blood came. Still holding Kobuk, she struggled to her feet and started back down the trail toward Tarnigan.

An eternity later, she felt something brush her shoulder and knew she had reached her destination. The effort of carrying Kobuk had warmed her blood until she tingled. She laid the half-conscious malamute down, felt her way to the nearest spruce tree, and wormed her way underneath the branches that fell to the ground. Not much space beneath them, but no snow had seeped through. She worked her way back out and, with a lot of grunting and shoving, managed to get Kobuk into the shelter. She stopped to rest just long enough to pat him and murmur words of encouragement.

"I'm not deserting you," Sasha told him. "I have things to do." She must have light enough to examine her dog's wounds. Using her gloved hands as a shovel, she scooped aside debris and needles and dug a small hole in the dirt beneath. She felt her way to the trunk of the tree and gashed out a few splinters with her knife, carefully stacking them in the hole. "Can't let it get too big," she muttered. "I don't want to burn up our night's accommodations."

Quick slashes of the knife severed the smallest branches and gave her fuel. A quick strike of the match later, a tiny fire spurted. She fed it sparingly and used its glow to examine Kobuk. If only Father were here. If she had needle and thread, she'd sew up the cut in the malamute's head. She'd often helped Nicolai.

"Please, God," she prayed. "Take care of us and help Naleenah and Father come soon."

By the time Sasha finished caring for Kobuk, now next to her with half-closed eyes, the storm had increased its intensity. New snow bent tree branches even lower. She checked her cut leg and found it no more serious than she'd expected. Sasha carefully put her matches inside her parka, packed the waterproof container with snow, and waited for it to melt. She held the precious drops in the palm of her hand and rejoiced when Kobuk's pink tongue feebly lapped them up.

A small piece of chocolate became supper, followed by a handful of snow that Sasha let melt in her mouth. The miniature fire added more cheer than warmth and when Sasha felt herself growing drowsy, she reluctantly let it die. She curled up with the dog in her arms and sleepily told him, "You're better than an extra parka."

Hours later, she had no idea how long, she awakened, shivering in every part of her body. "Kobuk?" she called. No answering bark came. Sasha forced her eyelids open. A tiny bit of light confirmed her suspicions. She lay alone in the makeshift shelter. Kobuk had deserted her.

"He would *never* do that." She squirmed out from under the tree. Unbroken white lay before her.

"Kobuk?"

Not even an echo came. She remembered Kobuk's head wounds. Certainty came, so strong Sasha staggered. The dog she loved had not failed her. In the way of the wild, he had gone off to die.

Chapter 9

Bern Clifton reached the Klondike well in advance of most of the human horde that swarmed out of Seattle in the fall of 1897. Fresh from his years in the north, his leg and arm muscles powerfully developed, he again proved the truism, "He travels swiftest who travels alone." Others tarried to equip themselves, to sell businesses, or tell families good-bye. Bern headed north and east, straight toward the already legendary source of riches.

He sometimes wondered if fate, which had dealt him such telling blows a few years earlier, had repented of her capricious ways. "Lady Luck" smiled on him shortly after he reached his destination. A chance encounter, if it really were chance, ended with Bern using his finest medical skills under primitive conditions to save a man's leg and probably his life. Bern found Kayak Jim, so named according to a scrawled paper on a handhewn table, lying on a cot in a rude hut. Fever sky-high from an improperly cared-for pickax wound to his foot, he raved like a maniac. Crimson streaks starting up his leg warned Bern. Blood poisoning had already begun its deadly work.

For three days he stayed with the prospector, tending him like a baby. He also cleaned up the shack. Gradually the fever receded. The angry crimson disappeared. When Kayak came to, he swore and wanted to know, "Who're you?"

"Dr. Bern Clifton."

"What in blue blazes are you doin' here? I ain't seen a sawbones since I struck pay dirt and had me a time in Vancouver a coupla years ago." The patient raised himself on one elbow. "Gimme a drink, will you?"

"Water only. No stimulants for a while," Bern ordered.

"Water! Stuff ain't good for nothin' 'cept makin' coffee and washin', and you gotta be careful about doin' too much of that." Kayak tried to swing his legs off the cot, then flopped back. "Weaker than a newborn colt. Say, how long've I been out?"

"Three days."

A strange expression came to the grizzled face. Fear leaped into his eyes. "What'd you do to this place?" he asked suspiciously. "There ain't been no other jaspers nosin' around, have there?"

"I cleaned it up. Couldn't stand the mess. No one else has come. Why should they?" Bern glanced around the hut and laughed. "I don't see anything worth stealing."

Kayak's eyes gleamed and he grunted. He drank the water Bern brought him, made a horrible face, and shuddered. "That stuff could kill a man."

Bern just laughed. In spite of the rough exterior, he rather liked the prospector. He found it next to impossible to convince Kayak he couldn't leap out of bed and get on with his search for gold. Finally he lost patience.

"Stop your bellyaching, will you? If I hadn't come along, you'd be whittling out a wooden leg to replace the one I saved, *if* you were lucky enough to be alive. Not to mention freezing or starving to death," he added.

"Is that the straight goods?" Keen eyes peered from under a tangle of sandy, graying eyebrows that matched Kayak's hair.

"Straight goods."

The prospector didn't answer for a long time. When he did, he sounded subdued. "I reckon I owe you."

"Forget it." Again Bern swept the cabin with an amused glance. "Doesn't look like you have anything I want for a fee. Besides, I helped myself to your grub when I ran out. I didn't dare leave you and go hunt for more."

"How old're you, Doc?"

"Thirty-one come December 31."

"I'm forty-seven and look sixty. That's what this here country does to you."

Bern didn't comment.

"You don't talk like nobody I ever knew." Kayak scratched his head with a bony forefinger. "How come you be up here back of beyond?"

Bern had no intention of spilling his life story to a stranger. He shrugged. "Why is the whole world coming here? Gold, pure and simple."

"They ain't a-gonna find it." A crafty look crept into the weather-beaten face. "Most the good claims done been took. 'Course, if a feller knows where to look . . ." He let his voice trail off.

"I'll bet you do."

The random shot paid off. Excitement as glittering as the dust men craved sent a

162

wave of color into Kayak's countenance. "You're pretty smart, Doc, but you're plumb wrong about there bein' nothin' of value here. See those sacks in the corner?" He pointed. "Lift 'em up."

Bern's pulse quickened at the mysterious note in his patient's voice. It slowed when he discovered nothing but the hard-packed dirt floor. "Nothing here."

"Get my tools and dig."

Fifteen minutes later Bern unearthed a rusty tin box, its hasp held with a file. It felt heavy.

"Open it."

His heart thumped. He pulled the file free with a screech that set his teeth on edge and lifted the lid, gasped, blinked, and looked again. A multitude of nuggets and a leather bag filled with gold dust filled every available inch of space. Kayak cackled. "Never seen nothin' like that, have you, Doc?"

"Never." Bern couldn't take his gaze from the contents of the box. "There's a fortune here!"

"Yup, and more where that come from."

Bern's blood burned. His head spun. Was this the lure of gold he'd heard about? The desire to possess more and more, the never-to-be-satisfied fever that raged in men's hearts and drove them to risk all for the yellow metal? He forced himself to close the box and set it on the table. "Why did you show me this?"

Kayak heaved his bad leg to a more comfortable position. He touched it significantly with a gnarled finger. "I reckon this is worth just about half of what's in the box. Fair enough?"

"Fair? Man, I can't take that kind of fee!" He stared at Kayak.

"Like I said, there's plenty more where it come from." The older man hesitated.

"I got me a claim back away from other folks' where they ain't any pryin' eyes to see what I take out. What's in the box come from there. The way I figure, 'twon't be long afore I get found out. Now if I had me a pardner, we might just get it cleaned up and vamoose with a couple pokes of gold."

"You're offering me interest in your claim?"

"Whadda you want, a written invitation?" Kayak scowled fearfully. "Doc, I'da never said anythin' 'less I meant it. Are you in or out?" He held out one hand. "Anyone what knows me can tell you Kayak Jim's handshake's better'n a contract."

"You'll trust me that much?" Bern marveled, thinking of those who hadn't.

The prospector snorted rudely. "Naw, I'm just shootin' the breeze to keep cool. Look, Doc, nobody said you had to stay here and take care of me, did they? What good's gold if I ain't alive to spend it, or if I'm stumpin' around on a hunk of wood? You're a good sawbones, but you're sure mule-dumb about folks!"

Bern let out a bellow of laughter loud enough to be heard in the Arctic. He stuck out his hand and shook Kayak's brown paw. "You don't know the half of it," he chortled. "Put her there, pard!" Not since the halcyon days of his friendship with Arthur had he let anyone get beneath the protective shell he'd developed. Now a crude prospector had seen through him and smashed the shell in one unexpected, unbelievably generous move.

As soon as Kayak Jim's leg healed, the two surreptitiously made their way to the rich claim. Day and night they worked, with one of them always on guard, until word leaked out that Bern was a doctor. From that moment, he alternated between helping Kayak on the claim and taking care of those who came to him.

Weeks passed into months. Still the vein held out. The pokes Kayak predicted grew heavy. He and Bern took to hiding them in different places. "Stands to reason if some ornery skunk searches and finds one cache, he won't think there's another," he philosophically stated. He also ordered Bern to wear ragged clothes and never show more than a little dust in the growing city of Dawson.

At last the vein petered out, but not before it had made the owners rich.

"Whadda you aim to do?" Kayak asked one evening in autumn. A whorl of pipe smoke ascended from the chair where he lounged. The pair had made a snug cabin from the tumble-down shack. "I'm hankerin' for the city. What say we head for Vancouver afore the snow flies?"

"Not me. I haven't lost anything there." Bern absently stroked the head of the husky who lay beside his chair. He had rescued Tong from a drunken miner bent on beating the dog to death, tended his wounds, and seen him slowly return to superb health. "I'm hankerin' to do more doctorin'," he said in an exact imitation of his friend.

"Here? I thought you'd got enough of patchin' up folks who ain't got the sense the good Lord gave 'em."

"I am. If I never take care of another

166

knife wound or gunshot from a senseless fight it will make me happy. The rush brought a few doctors along with a lot of other folks, so I'm not needed here so badly. I want to go where I am. I won't have to worry about money, thanks to you."

"Just where you fixin' on goin'?" Kayak half-closed his eyes.

For some strange reason, memory of Bern's interview with the perceptive doctor years before came to mind. *If I were thirty years younger . . . didn't have a family . . . Alaska Territory . . . plenty of elbow room . . . a handful of doctors . . . a practice that encompasses five hundred, maybe a thousand miles . . . small towns where people die when they don't need to.*

A stirring of excitement comparable to the moment when he first saw Kayak Jim's gold fired Bern's blood.

"Kayak, I'm going to Alaska Territory. I want to be under the Stars and Stripes again."

"Alaska?" Kayak peered at him. "Not such a bad idee. Blamed if I ain't tempted to tag along, s'posin' you want me, that is. We've pulled in harness pretty good this last year. I reckon anything that's in Vancouver'll still be there after I see

Alaska." An unaccustomed wistfulness sounded in his gruff voice.

"Nothing could please me more." Bern leaped up so quickly the toe of his boot prodded Tong. The husky scrambled to his feet and barked. His master patted him and he subsided. Bern sat back down. "We have to decide where to go. A man I once knew said Alaska Territory is one bi–i–i–g country."

"By the powers, I know just the place." Kayak's eyes gleamed. "I ain't never been there, but I talked to a feller who had. There's a village in north central Alaska near the Endicott Mountains. A fur trader named Nicolai Anton runs a trading post there. The Indians call him 'White Father.' Seems Anton treats 'em fair, practices what he preaches, which is outa the Good Book."

Bern grimaced. "Sounds like another hypocrite trying to get rich off the natives." He'd seen plenty of them in his years in the north and despised them all. Sometimes he wondered if it were because of his mixed blood.

"Anton's got the name for bein' different. Anyway, there ain't no doc for a million or more miles." Kayak grinned. "I hear Anton's got a daughter who's prettier than the name Tarnigan." Mischief flashed in his eyes.

"Deliver me from some female do-gooder! If I thought I'd have to associate with one, I'd go anywhere but Tarnigan."

"If she's dedicated to helpin' the Indians, she won't have time for hangin' around our cabin," Kayak dryly reminded.

"You win. Tarnigan, it is. Can we beat winter if we go now? I can be ready by day after tomorrow."

"Mayhap." The laconic answer was all Bern could get out of his partner.

Months later, Bern climbed up a steep, unfamiliar hill, exulting in his ability to do so. In spite of his athletic prowess, his speed on track and field, the mountains of Alaska had challenged him beyond endurance when he faced their inscrutable grandeur. He'd never dreamed anything could be so magnificent, so awe-inspiring. Peak after peak jutted higher than the one before and frowned down on a land most of civilization did not comprehend.

Neither Kayak Jim nor Tong had accompanied him. Snow had come earlier than they expected and dogged their entire journey from Dawson. They changed course and headed for Fairbanks, not really thinking they would make it.

"We did, but at a terrible cost," Bern whispered. The avalanche that swept the faithful Tong away tumbled Kayak Jim into a broken heap. What miracle saved himself Bern still didn't understand. If his father were there, he would have said it had been the hand of God. Bern could almost hear his father's voice telling him there must be a reason. Dad believed most people were allowed to remain on earth until they finished the work God gave them. In any event, Bern did what he could for Kayak. Somehow he got him to Fairbanks, knowing a power beyond himself opened ways through seemingly impossible situations.

For months he stayed in Fairbanks, visiting Kayak daily. Finally the haggard man reared up on his hind legs, figuratively speaking, and barked, "Don't be hangin' around here any longer. Go do your doctorin'. There's nothin' you can do here a dozen others can't do as well. I'll come when I get well. Go to Tarnigan and tell Nicolai Anton that Kayak Jim'll be along soon as he can, by summer for sure."

At last he extracted Bern's promise. Now high atop the lonely hill, Bern faced the truth. He no longer enjoyed traveling alone. He'd grown used to Kayak, to his droll speech and clear way of sorting life out. He missed the easy give and take between them, the matching of wits. Sometimes it reminded him of Arthur.

His years in the north had lessened his bitterness toward his one-time friend, especially after he told Kayak the whole story one snowbound evening in a trapper's deserted hut.

"You say he give up the gal and the job?" Kayak wanted to know through a cloud of pipe smoke.

"Yes."

"I reckon he couldn't do much more to show you he was sorry for bein' a fool."

The words haunted Bern. In time he even accepted them.

If only Arthur hadn't betrayed him! How they'd have climbed and struggled together. He could almost hear the blond man's joyous laughter ringing in the still air, echoing down white crevasses and into the great dark cloud on the far edge of the illimitable horizon. *Where was Arthur now? Did he, too, regret the insurmountable wall between them?*

Bern shook his fur-clad shoulders and pulled the hood of his parka higher. He wouldn't be here if Arthur had played fair.

Julia's face came to mind, as it had a hundred times in the six years since he left Philadelphia. His heartbeat continued at its normal rate. The girl he had worshiped meant less to him than one snowflake in a blizzard. She had freed him from enslavement in their last fatal interview. Not even her vindictiveness in making sure he didn't get the medical position rankled him. He wouldn't trade his life now for all the jewels in the world. Not for Julia or the finest appointment in the world. The great white north accepted a man for what he was, not who he was.

He shook off the past and faced the present. Lost in thought, he hadn't noticed how the black cloud so far away had come closer. He must find shelter. No chance of making it to Tarnigan even though, according to the crude map he and Kayak had drawn, it couldn't be more than a few miles distant. He ran his hand over his raspy chin. He'd been so intent on reaching the trading post, he hadn't shaved for three days.

Bern quickly surveyed the area. The top of the ridge caught the full force of the rising wind and he immediately rejected it. He strode downward until he reached a more sheltered spot where trees offered protection. Before the storm hit, he had found a large, overhanging rock, perfect for his purposes. It served as back wall and ceiling for the snow cave he hastily constructed. A well-regulated fire at the entrance warmed him without melting his temporary home. He whittled small pieces off his last chunk of jerky and warmed a single bannock. He had grown accustomed to the taste of these thin griddle-cooked flour cakes.

"I'm hungry for something besides this," he acknowledged. Deep in his soul he knew he hungered even more for companionship. Would he find it in Tarnigan, perhaps from Nicolai Anton? Certainly not from his daughter. Julia Langley's taunt remained as clear as the day she had spoken it. *No decent woman would even consider such a thing.*

Bern's jaw set in the familiar hard line. He would have no part of the other kind. There had been opportunity, plenty of it. Painted girls who haunted the gold camps brazenly sought his company. He scorched them with a glance and they bothered him no more. Neither had he dishonored himself by toying with the Indian girls, as so many did.

"At least my father married Crying

Dove," he told Kayak the one time he opened his heart and confessed his background. He couldn't yet think of her as Mother. "I didn't appreciate it when Dad said so. I do now."

"It's a wicked world, son," Kayak Jim observed. He let a heavy hand fall on the young doctor's shoulder. "I've done my share of ornery things, but I never have and won't treat women as anythin' but ladies, whether they d'serve it or not!"

Safe and cozy in his shelter, Bern grinned. "Sure hope Kayak's well enough to make it to Tarnigan this summer," he mumbled. Pillowing his head on his arms, he fell asleep.

The next morning he beheld a land strangely changed by the night's snowfall. He struggled to the top of a hill, but every step cost him. The soft white stuff tugged at his feet and weighed him down. No use trying to get to Tarnigan. It looked like another storm was on its way. Bern checked his dwindling supplies. He could hold out for a day or two. He crawled back in his shelter. The second storm hit. Once he thought he heard a voice calling but knew from long experience the tricks the wind so fiendishly plays.

By the next day, Bern realized he had to

get to Tarnigan. Lack of food had begun to take a toll even on his magnificent strength. He used the last of his flour to make a single bannock. Only a mouthful of jerky remained. Better to save it until he could go no farther.

A new worry came just before dusk. A mournful howling sent chills down his spine. He caught sight of a huge wolf pack on a ridge some distance away. Bern knew wolves seldom attacked humans, wild tales to the contrary. Yet the winter had been long, and food was in short supply. "Thank God for rifle and revolver." He realized what he'd just said and grinned. It slowly faded. With such a large number in the pack, could he bring down enough in rapid order should they choose to attack? He wished he'd remained in his shelter. The rock at his back meant animals couldn't sneak up on him.

"Some choice, starve or be attacked if they find my trail," he grimly said. No use trying to outrun the pack if the howling came nearer. He stopped where he was and prepared to make a stand. A flashing knife severed branches. A pitchy limb served as kindling. Five minutes later Bern had a roaring fire.

"That should keep them back. Tong, I

wish you were here." Thoughts of the great husky that would fight with his last drop of blood for his master brought mist to the dark eyes. The dog had become part of him, along with Kayak Jim.

Bern's keen ears picked up a new sound. His straight eyebrows drew together. Strange, it sounded more like a low whine than a wolf's howl. He readied his rifle and laid his pistol where he could snatch it up when needed. Through the dusk he saw something move toward him. Trigger finger steady, he waited.

A second whine stopped him. A gray and white beast bellied across the snow.

"You're no wolf!" Bern laid aside his rifle and held out one hand. "But what are you? Why is your head so lumpy?"

The animal stopped. Bern could hear it panting, as though it had run for miles. *Was this a mad dog? Did he dare approach it?* He strained his eyes against the lowering gray afternoon. A piece of stained cloth half on, half off the dog's head told the tragic story.

The physician in him that had never permitted Bern to pass anything injured overrode caution. He strode to the bound animal, saw the distinctive malamute markings, the pain-glazed blue eyes.

"Where did you come from?"

Too worn even to whine, the dog lay as one dead. Bern snatched off the blood-stained cloth and examined the wound. "Needs sutures." Taking the precaution to bind the malamute's jaws shut with the bloodstained cloth, he stitched the wound and freed him.

"Looks like you've lost a lot of blood, old man." He rebandaged the beautiful head. "What I can't figure is, who patched you up? Maybe it wasn't the wind I heard night before last. Is someone else out here in as big trouble as we are?"

A pink tongue protruded and feebly licked his helper's hand. The next instant a wolf howled. The hair on the malamute's neck rose. He tried to stand, but his legs gave way.

Bern cupped snow in his hands and the dog licked at it. The cry of a wolf, closer now, reached the man's listening ears.

"We're in for it." He looked around for a place to stash the injured dog and settled for lifting him under a tree with low-hanging branches.

"Stay," he ordered.

The wolves howled no longer. Bern wished they would. Silence menaced even more than the voice of the pack. He readied himself. A snowy bush to his right rustled and he turned toward the sound. Twin green lights flicked on, then off.

Close beside them, another pair winked, then others. Bern sent a lightning glance in the half-circle beyond his fire and counted ten pairs of eyes. One gaunt animal, bolder than his mates, crept into rifle range. Extreme hunger dulled fear of his age-old enemy — fire. Bern got him in his sights and waited. He couldn't afford to waste shots due to poor visibility. Now. He shot. The beast fell. Snarling and fighting, the pack leaped on their fallen companion. The sight sickened Bern, but he held steady. All too soon they'd leave their spoils. He'd be ready.

The snarls died. Emboldened by the taste of blood, the wolves inched closer. Bern thanked God for the steady nerve developed for the delicate operations in Philadelphia an eon ago. He waited as long as he could and fired twice. Two more wolves were brought down. Throwing the empty rifle aside, he grabbed his revolver, took aim, and pulled the trigger. It misfired. A brushing from behind warned him. A snarling beast rushed past, so close it hit Bern's shoulder and shoved him off balance. He took a snap shot, missed, and sagged with relief.

Roused from his stupor by the instinctive need to protect those he served, the wounded malamute had silently crept from shelter and launched himself at the clamoring pack.

Chapter 10

A mighty cry burst from Bern's throat, a tribute to the wounded malamute that had joined the fight. He aimed his revolver, taking care not to hit his unexpected ally. Of the four shots remaining, two scored. All but one of the remaining wolves howled and raced into the crouching night. That one and the dog lay locked in mortal combat. Bern grabbed his empty rifle and jacked a shell into the chamber. He ran as close to the pair as he dared. *He must not miss.* The weakening dog's life, possibly his own, rested in the shot. With an unconscious prayer for deadly accuracy, he fired. A convulsive quiver went through the gaunt frame. The wolf's hold lessened and he slid from the body of his nearly exhausted enemy.

"Thank God!" Bern cleared the short distance between him and the malamute in a single bound. He gathered the dog in his arms and raced back to the fire with him.

With trained, exploring hands he uncovered several gashes and quickly dressed them.

"You're going to make it, Dog," he promised. "You did tonight what few others would do." He glanced around. Dare he try to make Tarnigan tonight? Bern reluctantly shook his head. Better to let the dog rest. Filled with gratitude, he quickly threw together a lean-to from the brush and laid the tired animal inside. Next he heated water, then carefully measured and chipped up half of the last remnants of jerky and dropped them in the boiling water to soften. His mouth watered, but he sternly shook his head.

"This isn't for me. I can make it without. The other half of the jerky is for you in the morning." Bern blew on the mixture until it cooled, then he fed the nourishing broth with its bits of meat to the dog. A thrill went through him when a pink tongue licked his hand. He patted the beautiful head and looked deep into the blue eyes.

"Tomorrow, we'll go home."

Home? The word jarred and Bern's lips twisted. What a strange thing to say. He hadn't found a place to call home since he left Philadelphia. Long after he reloaded his weapons and dragged the wolf carcasses away from his meager camp, he wondered about it. Had Kayak Jim's tales of Tarnigan and the Antons made more of an impression than he'd realized? How ironic it would be if Dr. Bernard Clifton found a home in the vastness of this northern land.

The weary malamute had curled against Bern's left side and slept as one dead. Rifle and revolver lay at the man's right hand. He doubted what was left of the pack would be bold enough to return, especially now that they knew the enemy force had doubled. Still, he couldn't be sure. He dozed, then awakened and pitched more wood on the fire without disturbing his canine companion.

A stealthy sound roused him from the twilight between sleep and waking. Bern clutched his revolver and sat up.

"Who's there?" The clear, sharp call roused the dog, which leaped erect and snarled. Renewed by food and sleep, he hurled out of the lean-to, past the fire, and into the menacing dark. Bern sprang after him. No matter what danger lay in the blackness, the malamute must not face it alone. He grabbed the revolver with his right hand, his rifle with the left, and followed the dog.

Moments later, the growling changed to a frenzy of delighted barking. Bern's new companion reappeared at the edge of the firelight circle accompanied by a limping, parka-clad figure.

"Who are you?" Bern demanded, hands steady on his rifle.

The figure gasped and threw back the hood that hid its face.

Bern saw disheveled black braids, a pair of dark eyes, and a white face that belonged as little to this time and place as summer wildflowers. He lowered his revolver.

"A girl? How — where — what are you doing here? Where did you come from? Where is your sled, your dogs?"

She stumbled closer to the fire.

"I am Sasha Anton of Tarnigan." Her voice resembled shaken music, a songbird in a willow thicket. She fell to her knees beside the malamute and threw her arms around him. "Oh, Kobuk, I thought you had gone off to die!" She raised her head and looked at Bern. Bright tears glistened in the firelight. "Afternoon before last my friend Naleenah and I went for a run. She saw the storm cloud coming and called out. I looked back and didn't see the danger. Part of the trail had fallen away,

183

leaving a deep hole covered with a thin ice coating. Kobuk, the other dogs, our sled, and I fell in." She gingerly touched one leg. "Kobuk must have hit his head on the sharp rocks in the bottom of the hole. I hurt my leg and the sled broke. I sent Naleenah back with the other dogs to get help." She shivered. "I don't know why they haven't come. I took care of Kobuk as best I could." Her eyes opened wider. "You fixed the bandage?"

"Yes. I sutured him, too. He was about all in when he reached me. The wolf fight didn't help things —"

"Wolf fight!" Sasha's face turned even paler. "Kobuk was in no condition to fight wolves." She hugged her dog again.

"He did, though." Bern quickly told her how the malamute had helped even the odds after the revolver misfired. "So this is the second night you've been out? Did you have food?"

"Some chocolate." She rose and licked her lips. A faint smile curved them upward and touched Bern to the heart he'd thought was long dead.

He looked from her to the dog, wondering which needed sustenance more. Another glance at the swaying girl decided him, as did a short bark from Kobuk.

Sorry, old boy, he mentally apologized. *She needs it more than you.* "I have a little jerky left. I'll fix it for you."

She nodded and sank onto the floor of the open-sided lean-to, her feet extended toward the fire. Kobuk bellied over and stretched full length beside her.

It didn't take long to prepare the meager meal. While Bern worked, Sasha talked. "All day yesterday I waited. Once I thought I heard someone and I called, but no one answered." Her brow wrinkled. "I can't imagine why Father hasn't come, or Ivan."

"Ivan?"

"My father's assistant. He runs the trading post." She gratefully accepted the cup of jerky broth he handed her. "Naleenah surely got back to the village before the storm struck." Anxiety painted shadows beneath her drooping eyelids.

"It was tough going yesterday," he reminded.

"I know. I started toward home, but my leg ached and I kept sinking into the snow, so I went back under the spruce branches and stayed there." She sighed, half-asleep from the warm fire and broth. "When I heard shots, I knew someone had come for me, but it took a long time to get here.

185

How did you happen to be at this exact place?" She yawned. "Perhaps God sent you. . . ."

"You need to rest, Miss Anton. I was on my way to Tarnigan." He recoiled at the idea of being a messenger of the God he had not yet come to terms with in all the years since he left the East Coast. "First, I need to look at that injured leg." He liked the way she said, "All right," and turned a trusting gaze toward him.

How different from Julia! If caught in these circumstances — which he couldn't imagine her ever being — she'd simper and protest against even a doctor examining her leg. Not so this child of the wild. She simply watched his every move and barely flinched when he probed the wound and dressed it with a healing lotion, one which he knew smarted. Kobuk eyed the whole process from between slitted lids with one of Sasha's hands tangled in his ruff as if she never wanted to let him go.

"Sleep, Miss Anton."

"Sasha." Her eyes closed, then popped open. "I don't even know your name, but you're a good doctor. A real one?"

"Yes. Dr. Bernard Clifton, Bern to my friends."

A trill of laughter brought an answering

smile to his stern lips. "It fits, you know. Bernard means 'brave bear.' " She yawned again. This time her eyelids stayed shut. Soon her soft breathing showed that she slept.

For hours, Bern hunkered under a blanket next to the fire, thinking deep thoughts. *Could this chance encounter be more than that? Had the hand of God actually led him to this place?* His mind rejected the idea. His heart did not. Far from so-called civilization, a man either found and accepted life as more than what he made it or gave way to the base elements always ready to claim him. Desperate men roved the north, heads ever turning from what lay before them to the fear and shame of dark deeds behind. *What if he were such a man?* He shuddered. Better for Sasha Anton to have died in the snow.

She stirred restlessly and curled closer to Kobuk. Bern wondered if she were cold. He unhesitatingly stripped the blanket from his shoulders and tucked it around her prone figure, aware of the malamute's gleaming eyes and suddenly tense body. Even with the beginnings of friendship between them, Bern knew a single threatening move toward the girl would send Kobuk straight for his throat. He fiercely rejoiced at the thought. So long as she had the dog, no man could harm her.

He formulated his plans and, with the earliest streaks of light, quietly began to carry them out. By the time Sasha awakened, Bern had already built what he called a "wilderness ambulance," a travois-like sledge on which Sasha and Kobuk could ride. Recognizing his weakened condition from exposure, lack of food, and little sleep, Bern grimly determined he'd haul them to Tarnigan if it killed him.

A half-hour later they set out. Despite Sasha's protests, her rescuer flatly refused to let her walk even part of the way.

"You'll only slow us down," he told her and lunged ahead, the rope taut between him and the sled.

Step after dogged step, he pulled his passengers forward. A light snow sifted down and he worked harder. Yet the time came when he knew he couldn't go much farther. Breasting the storm, Bern came to the top of a hill. Had he gone snow-blind? Dartles and sparkles swam before his eyes.

"Tarnigan. Bern, we've made it." Sasha's simple statement sent a final burst of energy through the fatigued doctor. He started down, down, toward the lighted windows of the village.

Memory of other lighted windows came. He laughed. Once he thought he knew what they meant: a waiting father, warmth, cheer. Here in this desolate land they spelled a different message. Life itself lay behind those lighted windows. For the second time, he had a feeling of coming home.

Ever afterward, Bern remembered his entrance to Tarnigan as a series of blurry events. A weeping, beautiful Indian girl met them at the Anton door.

"Sasha, I failed you," she cried, her slim hands busily undoing the other's outdoor clothing.

"Never mind, Naleenah." Sasha cut short the explanation. "I have to get into dry clothing. So does Dr. Clifton, who saved me. We're starving and so is Kobuk. Where is Father?"

Too distraught to heed Sasha's protests, Naleenah said, "That's what I'm trying to tell you." She clasped her hands together and twisted them. "The fur cache was robbed the afternoon we went out. Father and Ivan had already gone on the trail of the thieves by the time the dogs and I returned. The white men I could trust had gone with them." She choked. "I went to the Indian village. Even though my father

189

had sold me, I thought Tonglaw would help me find you." A black, masklike shadow came over her face and dulled her wet eyes.

"The encampment raged with shouting men and screaming women. I crept closer. Tonglaw and the braves were mad with firewater. The women and children fled into the forest for safety. I dared not go farther. I heard men calling my name, cursing Tonglaw for allowing Nicolai Anton to adopt me. I dared not think of what would happen should they find me. Somehow, I managed to get home. I knew the stout walls of *Nika Illahee* would protect me. I barricaded the door and blew out the lamps. Then I took a knife from the kitchen."

Sheer terror sprang to Naleenah's dark eyes. "I know it is wrong to kill, but all I could remember was how white men treated the women of my tribe. They came, cursing and shouting. I remained still. At last, they left." She shivered as if she were dripping with snow and not the new arrivals.

"Oh, Naleenah, what a terrible thing!" Sasha blanched.

"The next day and night the drunkenness continued. I dared not try to come for you with a sled and leave tracks for them to follow. I feared for what might happen to you as well as me."

"No one would dare lay a hand on Nicolai Anton's daughters," Sasha exclaimed.

"Drunken men know no rules," Naleenah said. "I stayed inside, all day and night. Gradually the sounds from the encampment ceased. Still I could not venture out. Surely Father, Ivan Romanov, and the others would come soon." She turned her face toward Bern. "Thank God for sending you to find her and bring her home."

He squirmed under her praise. "Kobuk is actually the hero. We'll tell you the story later." His teeth chattered, yet for some reason he felt burning hot. "I think I'd better sit down." He took a step toward the nearest chair and felt himself falling into a black pit that offered no escape.

A babble of voices intermittently rang in his mind. Ghostly faces haunted him. Arthur and Julia. Dad and Dr. Langley. Kayak Jim. Tong — no, he was dead, wasn't he? Bern raved incoherently, accusing them of treachery and keeping secrets. Yet his body resisted the fever, and he hung on to life by a thread no larger than the sutures he had used to stitch Kobuk's head.

Sasha seldom left his bedside. When she did, Naleenah took her place. Big Nicolai Anton shook his head when he returned from his unsuccessful quest the morning after Bern brought his daughter home. "He's a mighty sick man."

"You can't let him die," Sasha told him. "He saved Kobuk and me."

Nicolai caught the anguish in her face, rolled up his sleeves, and went to work with all the rude skill he'd learned. When the crisis approached, the trader told Sasha, "It is time to send the letter he carries."

"It says to send only upon his death," the faithful nurse protested. Her father's silence caused her to cry out, "He will not give up! His body is weak but his spirit still fights."

Nicolai said no more.

"He will not die," Naleenah comforted. "He is Hoots-Noo, 'heart of a grizzly.'"

Heartened, Sasha renewed her efforts, coaxing a few drops of medicine between his pallid lips.

One afternoon the patient opened his eyes.

"You fell ill," Sasha told him, a soft finger over his lips. There was no more he needed to know just now. "You are at *Nika*

Illahee, 'my dear homeland.' Don't try to talk." His mouth curled in the travesty of a smile that caught at her heart before he fell into a deep, healing sleep.

Once his temperature dropped, Bern made a remarkable recovery.

"Fine thing," he complained one day. "Me lying here being waited on by you girls. I'll be so spoiled Kayak Jim will throw up his hands and go back to gold mining when he gets here. I need to get out and into a place of my own." Yet a pang went through him. He had learned to love *Nika Illahee* in the short time he'd been there.

"Don't you feel welcome?"

"Of course." Bern silently amended his comment. One person had made it quite clear how unwelcome the doctor was, although never in the presence of others. Ivan Romanov, good-looking though he was, had a sneer that made Bern long to rearrange the manager's face. So did his remarks about which shacks in the village were available. Bern grinned. Ragamuffin he might look, but he could and would have a home built in Tarnigan along the style of the Antons'. He reveled in the knowledge he had the means to do so. Evidently Romanov had taken the same in-

193

stant dislike to the new doctor Bern felt the first time he saw the blond-haired man look at Sasha through half-closed eyes. How surprised Ivan would be to discover Bern could buy all of Tarnigan any time he wished.

Perhaps because of that mutual dislike, Bern noticed small incidents the others appeared to miss or ignore: a certain craftiness in Ivan's expression; the unconscious way he greedily flexed his fingers when the talk turned to riches. Suspicion grew. Bern laughed when it first came, and sobered the more he thought about it. What if Romanov knew more about the unpleasant happenings in the village and Indian encampment than the Antons realized? Even though the doctor attributed his feelings as a natural result of his hostility toward Ivan, he decided to keep a sharp watch on Ivan. If he really were involved in furnishing whiskey to the Indians, Anton would drive him out, regardless of the years he had served.

I have to be sure, Bern told himself. *No false accusations. One hint of such a thing and whoosh, the fox will streak to cover.*

A second and equally disturbing suspicion arose. If Romanov were running whiskey, he might also be involved in systematically robbing Anton's fur cache. Hot blood rose to Bern's face. He'd come to respect Nicolai. He owed Anton and his daughters his life. Only faithful care and nursing saved men as sick as Bern knew he had been. On the spot, he pledged himself to their service the way knights of old pledged themselves to their kings and fair ladies.

The third and final suspicion left Bern so shaken he couldn't believe even Romanov guilty. He had seen the look in Ivan's blue eyes when he looked at Naleenah.

The days became weeks. Clifton's home went up swiftly because of the good wages he offered to get it done as soon as possible. He'd moved into a small cabin as soon as the Antons reluctantly agreed. Bern saw less of Ivan now, but a chance meeting in the trading post confirmed his worst fears. Ivan might be in love with Sasha, but his eyes betrayed him when he gazed at Naleenah.

Bern wanted to cry out, to warn her of impending tragedy. Who knew better than he how such a situation could turn out? Nay, this would be far worse. Romanov might desire Naleenah, but he wouldn't marry her. Did the laughing Indian girl share Ivan's feelings? Bern couldn't be sure. He considered discussing his misgivings with Nicolai and shook his head. Making such a charge could result in no recourse but for him to leave Tarnigan, something he hoped he'd never have to do.

"It's home," he told a spring sky one afternoon on the way back to town from a visit to the Indian encampment. Ever since the swollen-jawed Tonglaw came to Bern at Nicolai's insistence, he'd been called to attend the Indians now and then. He grinned, remembering Tonglaw's yell of pain when the abscessed tooth came out and his terse comment, "Hoots-Noo good medicine man."

"I'm in love with this place," he told the waving willows and scudding clouds. *And Sasha,* they whispered.

"No!" Yet denying it at the top of his lungs didn't make it untrue. From the time he saw Anastasia Jeanne Anton stagger into his firelit camp and throw back her parka hood, he hadn't been the same man. He thought of how she cared for him when he was so ill. Sometimes he thought she had willed him back to life. Surely she had prayed for him. Now, weeks later, it came to him with the freshness of spring and clean air. He loved her, and it made what he once felt for Julia Langley less than nothing. Thankfulness rushed through him. *Suppose he had stayed in Philadelphia, married Julia, and never met Sasha.*

His heart missed a beat, then went on. Dad's constant reminder that God brought good out of all situations floated through his mind. He felt alive, stronger, and more invincible than he had since the long-ago day he stood on the pinnacle of success in Philadelphia.

Now he knew how little that past feeling had meant. Here, on the top of the world, he didn't lift his head arrogantly as he had once done. Instead, he bowed before the wondrous thing that had come into his life, humbled at how he had been spared the pain and disillusionment of marriage with Julia.

Marriage? He crashed to earth, his joy changing to fear. How would Sasha react when she learned he was half American Indian? "She has Indian blood, too," he muttered. "Nicolai said so. They're a mixture of French, Russian, and Indian." Yet doubts persisted. The native blood was a few generations old. Whatever caste system Tarnigan held he had no way of knowing. Always Julia's scathing denunciation that no decent woman would ever want him rankled his conscience.

Even if it makes no difference, why do you think you can win her? he asked himself. *There's Romanov to deal with, remember?*

Ivan's gaze at maid and mistress showed him unfit for either. Bern's face darkened. "He won't get her. Or Naleenah, either. I'll dig out the truth and turn it over to Anton. He will deal with it."

He reiterated the vow a few nights later when his diligent snooping disclosed Ivan sneaking around behind *Nika Illahee.* Bern's blood boiled. He saw Romanov pitch a few small stones at a window at the back of the house. *How dared he?* The doctor's stomach churned when the window opened and he slithered closer, protected by the darkness of night and trees near the house.

"No, Ivan. I've told you. I cannot betray Sasha and Father Nicolai."

"You know I love you."

Ivan's pleading voice lit flares of anger in the eavesdropper.

"Then stand before the missioner with me."

"Shhh. We don't want anyone to hear. I've told you I'll marry you. What difference does it make if you come to me now or then?"

"God says it makes a difference."

Bern wanted to cheer Naleenah's strength. Instead, he held his breath and listened even harder, unwilling to miss a single word of the low conversation.

"If you loved me, you would come."

"Ivan." A world of sadness rested in the reply. "If you really loved me, you wouldn't ask me to do something I believe is wrong."

"At least kiss me good night, Naleenah."

Bern felt rather than saw the merging of figures before Ivan stole away. He lay still until a sobbing breath and the closing of the window told him he'd learn no more that night. Thoughtful and glad Naleenah had not gone the way of so many Indian girls who fell in love with white men, he silently retraced his steps to his cabin. He spent the rest of the night wondering what Nicolai would say and do the next day when he learned of Romanov's treachery.

One thing — whatever happened, nothing must destroy Sasha and Naleenah's friendship. If only Nicolai could think of a way to prevent it. Late frost touched the world with icy, searching fingers, and daylight followed before Bern threw himself on his bed, dreading what the new day had in store.

Chapter 11

During the long night hours, Bern's mind raced like a caged beast. The trader obviously liked and trusted Romanov. Would he take the word of a newcomer against that of his trusted manager? It might be better to lay low, watch, listen, and see if Ivan were involved in other unsavory activities as well as the clandestine pursuit of Naleenah. A little voice inside whispered, *wait*. He awakened knowing the wisdom of that course.

A week passed. Another. Bern snatched sleep by day and watched by night. Ivan did no more night wandering. Had he taken Naleenah's refusal as final? Bern hoped so but doubted it.

Summer in all its northern loveliness spread over the land. Carpets of wildflowers nodded in the breeze. The sun smiled a benediction and Bern's spirits rose. He could not pinpoint the moment when the faith of his fathers crept back into his soul. He had come to realize, however, God had not changed, nor would He do so. The most trusted loved ones inevitably let others down in one way or another. God did not. Bern found himself singing snatches of hymns he'd learned in childhood while he went about his work. He purchased a sturdy horse from Tonglaw and thought nothing of traveling countless miles to bring comfort and healing to any who summoned him. His wide-ranging practice also furnished Bern with contentment, satisfaction, and an acute knowledge of the terrain. When winter returned, he could easily find the widely scattered people tucked away in the shoulders of the hills and mountains near Tarnigan.

Bern moved into his sweet-smelling log home with gladness and a sense of completion. With Nicolai's beaming permission, it sat on a low rise at the opposite end of the village, as near a replica of *Nika Illahee* as willing hands could make it.

One evening, Bern fell asleep smiling, only to awaken a few hours later. A feeling of urgency filled him, a nagging knowledge of something left undone. He lay quietly, thinking, until it came to him. "God," he said. "I know You've forgiven me. I've also

forgiven Arthur and Julia — and Dad." His
throat tightened. "I need to tell him."

Bern threw back the covers, made a
light, and sat down at a handcrafted table.
In short order, he filled several pages with
his bold, black scrawl — the first real letter
he'd sent in his six wandering years. What
it amounted to was a recitation of all that
had happened. He ended with these words:

God has given me nothing I dreamed
of and everything I need. If Sasha
Anton returns my love, I will be the
most blessed man who ever lived and
spend the rest of my life in Tarnigan.
Only after I realized love is so much
more than mere attraction could I
comprehend your feelings for my
mother. I wish I could have known her.
I see in an Indian girl here named
Naleenah what Crying Dove must
have been: good, beautiful, and strong.

Forgive me for my harsh judgment. I
was caught up in the excitement of
achieving success and did not understand. How I long to see you! My por-
tion of the fortune Kayak Jim so
generously shared has barely been
touched. I intend to speak with
Nicolai about building a church and

setting up a fund to get a good minister here. We desperately need one. The few missioners who come through have a parish a hundred times too large to spend enough time with us. Anton does his best, but there is so much evil and it's getting worse all the time. I see new silver streaks in Nicolai's hair from watching the mighty people he loves succumb to degrading influences.

How I long to see you! Perhaps one day I will come to Philadelphia. Or, God willing, He may allow you to come here. You would love it, as I do.

Bern stared at the page, signed it "Your loving son," and realized night had given way to a predawn murkiness. He started back to bed, then reconsidered. Restlessness twanged at him, an odd premonition of something not quite right. His years in the wilderness had long since taught him never to ignore such a feeling. He dressed, stuck his revolver in his belt, and grabbed his rifle in case a prowling beast had invaded Tarnigan. Outside, he paused, then resolutely turned toward *Nika Illahee*.

His hunch paid off. Keen eyes accustomed to peering long distances made out a hunched form at the Anton fur cache. Shuffling sounds warned another man was inside. Bern gasped. The big padlock hung loose. Suspicion flamed. It had been opened using the combination, not broken. Bern stayed out of sight. A bundle of pelts came flying through the cavernous doorway. Even in the morning dimness Bern could see they were the most precious of all: silver fox. The guard grunted, shouldered the bundle, turned, and trudged off toward the trading post.

The watcher heaved a sigh of relief at the sight of the brown face. He had feared it might be Tonglaw. Now what? If he followed the thief, the brave would drop the furs, outrun him, and be innocently asleep in the Indian encampment with no one the wiser. Bern wasn't positive he could identify him.

More shuffling signs demanded a decision. The man inside the cache would appear at any moment. Bern sneaked to the open door and gently lifted the padlock. Why must the thing screech? "What —"

The startled voice galvanized him to action. Bern threw himself against the door, slammed it shut, got the padlock in place, and snapped the lock shut just in time. A mighty blow told him the furious thief was battering against the solid door. Bern smiled. Let him batter. No man could get out of the prisonlike structure, and the present occupant wouldn't dare shout for help for fear of rousing the Antons.

His heart thudding like an Indian drum, Bern pondered his next move. He smiled again and paced back and forth in front of the cache on noiseless feet until daylight came with a howl of village dogs. When lights appeared in the Anton home, he headed for the front door and knocked.

"Why, Clifton!" Nicolai, still buttoning his shirt, looked astonished. "What are you doing out so early? Come in, man. Sasha, Naleenah, we have a hungry man here."

Bern's heart sank. He'd hoped to find Nicolai alone. On the other hand, perhaps this was better. They would discover the identity of the cache robber together.

"Bern?" Sasha came into the room with Naleenah at her heels. Early as it was, both girls were dressed in simple cotton gowns and had their hair braided. A look of dread crossed Naleenah's face, but Sasha glowed. "How nice! A breakfast visitor."

"I didn't come for breakfast. I have a thief locked in the fur cache."

"Wha–at?" Nicolai's roar broke in the middle.

"I got up early and felt restless." He described how he'd seen an Indian walk off with a bundle of silver fox pelts before he trapped a second man inside.

"Please." Naleenah held out a shaking hand. "The man outside, it was not —"

"A brave. I doubt if I'd know him from a dozen others."

The worry left Naleenah's eyes.

"What are we waiting for?" Nicolai stamped out, closely followed by the others. Giant steps took him to the cache. "Do you know who you shut up?"

Bern felt thankful he could honestly reply, "No." He didn't know and kept his suspicions that amounted to certainty to himself. "What surprised me was the padlock wasn't broken. Who knows the combination?"

Nicolai broke stride and whipped around toward him. "I do. So does Sasha. Ivan, of course." He looked puzzled.

"Anyone else?"

The shaggy head wagged back and forth. "I don't see how. You're sure it wasn't broken?"

"Positive." Bern's voice rang in the early morning air. "It slid right back in." He hesitated, knowing he needed to clinch the evidence against the trapped thief. "You're always sure you lock it, I suppose."

"Sure!" Sasha giggled, although her eyes looked scared. "He locks it, checks it, then just before bedtime, comes out and checks it again."

Nicolai looked sheepish. "Better to look a hundred times than leave it open once." The corners of his mouth turned down. "The first few years we were here, we didn't even own a lock. The infernal influence of greedy men has corrupted my people."

Before they reached the sturdy building, the sound of heavy blows reached them. The door didn't even creak from the attack. The ominous fact the temporary resident didn't speak confirmed Bern's conclusions.

"Stand back," Nicolai ordered in a voice that boded ill to the man inside. He spun the dial, jerked the padlock free, and swung the door open. "Come out with your hands in the air," he told the man crouched inside. A string of oaths issued from the depths of the cache.

"Hold your wicked tongue!" Nicolai bellowed. "There are ladies present and I don't stand for that kind of talk even if there weren't."

Bern expected a cringing trading post

manager, not the blustering, furious man who erupted like a long-sleeping volcano.

"Who locked me in?" he demanded.

His wild gaze traveled the group and then rested on Bern.

"You!" He clenched his hands into fists and flung himself at the doctor. "You meddling sawbones, I'll teach you to snoop into my business."

Nicolai's brawny arm shot out, grabbed his manager's shoulder, and stopped him.

"Suppose you tell us what you were doing in my fur cache."

The deadly note in his voice had a visible effect on the other. Ivan licked his lips and froze in place. "I brought over some pelts from the post," he sullenly said.

"What about the Indian who made off with a bunch of silver fox?" Bern demanded.

Ivan's gaze scorched him. "He must have been waiting. He hit me on the head after I opened the lock. When I came to, he was gone."

"Waiting at this hour?" Disbelief shone in Nicolai's face. "No one would expect you to be here before dawn."

In his eagerness to defend himself, Romanov made a fatal mistake. He tore free of Nicolai's gasp, then turned toward

Bern and cried, "Ask Clifton what he was doing here. I have more right to be at your cache than he does. He's after Sasha and is trying to get me in bad. Who are you going to believe? Someone who has served you faithfully for years or a miserable sneak who came out of nowhere? What do you really know about him? He could be a murderer or selling whiskey to the Indians. I wouldn't be surprised if he and the Indian had this plot all hatched up to discredit me and get away with a load of furs."

"That's enough, Ivan." Nicolai's command sliced like a fine hunting knife.

"Only three persons know the combination to the padlock. Stolen furs and whiskey to the Indians began long before the doctor came." His eyelids closed until only slits remained. "You've betrayed me, whether or not I can prove it. Pack and get out. Today."

"Before he goes you may wish to search his quarters," Bern put in.

A slight suggestion of foam came to Ivan's lips. "Don't count on a long life if you stay in Tarnigan, Clifton," he warned. A strange light glowed in his blue eyes, making them more glacierlike than ever. He looked at Sasha, then Naleenah, smiled curiously, and marched off.

Something in his parting glance sent shivers through Bern. While the girls fixed breakfast, he had a long talk with Nicolai.

"I hate to add to your troubles," he awkwardly began. "But I don't put it past Romanov to make one more move." He related the scene with Naleenah at the window and watched Anton age before his eyes.

"I should have seen it coming," the trader admitted, his brow furrowed. "I'm not often fooled, but Ivan has been like the son I never had. Now, what can we do?"

"Watch," Bern succinctly told him.

"Shall we tell the girls?"

"No. I'll stand guard outside. You be ready inside." He paused. "Where do you think Ivan might go?"

"Tonglaw brought word that a band of renegade Indians has pitched camp a few miles from here. If Ivan's been supplying whiskey to them — and it appears he has — they'll welcome him." Bern nodded, his mind busy with a hundred details. "If Romanov strikes, it has to be tonight. I suspect he will make a show of leaving and sneak back. I'll track him."

"Take Kobuk. Funny, the pup couldn't stand Ivan from the time I brought him to

Sasha." He shrugged. "Sometimes dogs are smarter than their owners."

That night Bern took up his post outside the windows at the back of *Nika Illahee*, taking care to stay in the shadows. A lopsided moon gave enough light to be seen. He thought of the malevolent look Ivan had cast his way when he made a final attempt to convince his employer of his innocence. A search of his premises had turned up no furs, but that didn't mean anything. Except for the bundle of pelts taken the night before, Ivan had had plenty of time to stash his loot elsewhere.

Nicolai hadn't given an inch. "Don't ever come back," he said. "There is no welcome in Tarnigan for a traitor. I cannot be responsible for what the men might do if your treachery becomes known." Ivan silently turned away, but the swing of his shoulders showed neither remorse nor defeat. Bern and Kobuk tracked him to the renegade encampment and back.

The sound of pebbles on Naleenah's window roused Clifton. He held his breath. The window stayed closed.

"Naleenah, open the window," came a low call. Nothing happened. Obviously determined to seek revenge, Ivan threw caution to the night wind. Something clicked

in his hand. Bern saw the gleam of moon-
light on steel. The knife blade slipped beneath the window and gently raised it.

"Naleenah?" Ivan pushed the window
higher, rested his hands on the sill, and
thrust his head inside.

"Ivan, what are you doing?" Not
Naleenah's frightened voice, but Sasha's,
crisp and demanding. A light flashed on.
From his vantage point, Bern could see
clearly: Ivan, his head still inside the open
window, Sasha, staring at the intruder, her
hands clutching her dressing gown, Naleenah, shrinking back from the window.

"What's carrying on in here?" Nicolai
Anton, fully dressed, bounded into the
room and to the window. He yanked Ivan
inside. "You sneaking cur! Isn't it enough
that you steal my furs? Would you rob me
of my most priceless possession as well?"

Ivan wrenched himself free and threw
back his golden head. "Not Sasha. You
killed any chance of her loving me." Corroding bitterness rang in his accusation.
"It's Naleenah I've come for. She loves me
and is going with me." Bern longed to fling
himself inside and throttle the confident,
smirking Romanov.

"Is this true?" Nicolai whirled toward
the girl.

"I love him." Her eyes changed to dark pools of misery. "I always have." Her head drooped, then came up with such pride and renunciation Bern blinked back mist. "I told Ivan I would go, but only after we stood before the missioner."

"Do you mean to marry this girl?" Nicolai thundered.

Ivan folded his arms. "Whites don't marry Indians."

All the indignities Bern had suffered rose in a wild tide of fury.

"Get out!" Anton raved. "Get out before I forget Almighty God's commandment not to kill and strangle you with my two hands. You would bring shame to my house and my daughter."

Naleenah ran to him with a cry like a wounded creature. One long arm encircled her. Nicolai's other hand pointed toward the door. Ivan's footsteps sounded loud until the slamming of the front door cut them off. "Child, you have done right." Anton patted the Indian girl's shining hair.

"I know, but Father Nicolai, it is so hard."

Bern could bear no more. He worked his way out of his place of concealment and followed Ivan clear to the renegade camp. Not until his quarry vanished into a tumbledown affair of mud, sticks, and stones did the shaken doctor head back to Tarnigan. Heavy of heart, he cried to the fading night, "Oh, God, why must such things be?" A pink dawn and peace stole into his soul at the same time. One day there would be no sin and heartache. Until then, everyone who believed had a duty to fight for right and truth, even harder than he fought against dirt and sickness, no furloughs granted.

Memory of Ivan's arrogance, "Whites don't marry Indians," kept step with him all the way home. Would the Antons feel that way, too? The need to know burned within him like an unquenchable fire. He dared not speak to Nicolai on such short acquaintance. Neither had Sasha ever given him anything but friendship. How could he go to either and explain the love he had for this flower of the north who made hothouse roses pale by comparison? No, only God would know — and Dad, when he received the letter a swift runner of the woods had already taken.

"Take care of your sister," Nicolai brokenly ordered when the front door slammed. He wheeled and went out of the bedroom.

Sasha had never felt more helpless or hurt. She ached inside from the terrible scene, yet knew what she experienced was nothing compared with Naleenah's pain. In the months to come, would the manner of Ivan's rejection aid in healing? Sasha's work with her father had taught the need to remove all traces of problems lest they fester and poison the blood. "Come. We will share my bed for the rest of the night." She led the unprotesting younger girl to her room, left a lamp burning low, and climbed into bed beside her friend. A long while later Naleenah said, "You are angry with me."

"Never!" Sasha realized her silence had been construed as criticism. "How could I be? I just wish I had told you all those months ago how Ivan acted toward me on my birthday. He was so fierce, so demanding." She quickly sketched in the scene. "Naleenah, love is more than that." She hesitated. Was it right to repeat what her father had said about her mother? A quick glance at her friend showed how badly she needed encouragement. In broken tones, she shared the story of a love so great it would always be spring in Nicolai's heart. "Someday such a love will come to us," she said. "Or if God does not will it, we will stay together always."

Unshed tears brightened Naleenah's dark eyes. "I knew Ivan Romanov didn't love me that way when he warned me not to tell you about us. I hoped it would come. I knew you cared for him the same way you love me, as a sister." She smiled, a forlorn little smile that made her face sadder than before. "Hoots-Noo loves you as Nicolai loved his Jeanne."

Hoots-Noo. Heart of a grizzly. Dr. Bernard Clifton. Sasha felt red banners fly to her cheeks. "Why, what makes you think that?"

"I have seen it in his eyes. Sometimes they shine like dark lava. Other times they are shadowed like beneath the great spruce trees."

"He has never even hinted at such a thing," Sasha protested. She turned her face away so Naleenah couldn't see the joy she knew had etched itself there.

"He has known great sadness. It shows in his face. He will not burden you with it unless he knows the kind of love Nicolai had for his Jeanne lives in your heart," the other girl said. "The love a woman has for the one she chooses to mate with for life."

"How do you know these things?" Sasha whispered.

"I, too, have suffered."

Sasha couldn't answer. She reached over, clasped her friend's hand, and fell asleep with a strange, new feeling in her heart.

The next morning she awakened before Naleenah. Sasha looked at the younger girl and sighed. How could she feel like singing when her Indian sister carried such a deep hurt? She quietly slipped from bed, dressed, and went to find her father. He sat on the divan, his face showing signs of turmoil.

"Little Flower, it is bad business," he somberly said when she sat down beside him.

"I know. What can I do to help Naleenah?"

"Surround her with your love. Our Father will heal her heart." Nicolai peered into his daughter's sparkling brown eyes. "Ivan did not hurt you, too, did he?"

"Only by his betrayal of Naleenah and us all." She did not want to talk about Ivan. "Father, do you think Bern — Dr. Clifton — l-likes me? A lot, I mean?" She had almost said loved. "Isn't that a strange question for a twenty-four-year-old woman to ask her father?"

"It is because you have little experience with suitors and their ways," he reminded.

His dark eyes flashed and a laugh rumbled in his chest. "Who better could you ask than the one who loves you more than life, second only to our Lord?"

"No one." She smiled.

"Do you wish for him to l–like you, a lot, Anastasia?" he mimicked.

"I don't know," she frankly told him. "He seems to be a fine man. Yet some of the hateful things Ivan said are in my mind. We really do not know much about him."

"We know he is man enough to risk exhaustion and his life to save my daughter and the dog who fought for him. We know he loves his God. Oh, yes," he added when she gave an involuntary start of surprise. "He has only recently rediscovered how much."

"Naleenah said there has been great sadness in his life," she irrelevantly put in. "I wonder what it is?"

"What else did Naleenah say?" Nicolai cocked his bushy head to one side.

Without a hint of self-consciousness she replied, "That he had love in his eyes for me but also sadness. That he wouldn't speak of it unless he knew I loved him the way —" She started to say, "You loved my mother," but hastily changed it to, "The way a woman loves the man she chooses to mate with for life."

"He is an honorable man, Little Flower. Do not fret or try to find love. Those who do chase only a will-o'-the-wisp. It must come to you in God's own time."

He heaved himself from his chair, stroked her dark hair, and went out whistling.

The sound bathed Sasha's troubled heart with gladness. For some obscure reason, their talk had lifted Nicolai's spirits. Soon she must go to the kitchen and prepare the morning meal. First, she needed strength to meet the day — and Naleenah.

Sasha bowed her head and whispered, "Please, God." She found herself unable to go on. She knew her heavenly Father understood her needs far more clearly than she herself, even more than the earthly father into whose arms her mother had laid her at birth. What need had He of words from one He had so lovingly created?

"Thank You, God," she finished. She sprang to her duties, made light by the happiness that bubbled inside her and had not been there the day before.

Chapter 12

Each sparkling day of the too-short summer season dawned on the north country in unsurpassed splendor. A hundred, nay, a thousand times Sasha longed to hold each one close. She couldn't remember waking other summer mornings with the anticipation that greeted her even before she opened her eyes. A new awareness of life itself crept into her heart. Love came on dainty fawn's feet, timid and soft. She knew the radiance that shone in her watery image when she bent to drink from icy streams gave her away to Nicolai and Naleenah. *How could Dr. Bern Clifton fail to see it?*

Perhaps he didn't. Rich red mantled her cheeks and her pulse quickened. Although he kept his dark gaze steady when they met, a few times she caught an unguarded glance. It held admiration, respect, and something she dared not name.

With the going of Ivan, the Indian encampment settled to its usual pace with only an occasional outburst of drunkenness. This in itself condemned Anton's former manager.

"How could he sink so low?" Sasha asked her father one sunny morning when Naleenah had gone to the trading post for a few supplies. They never discussed Ivan now. Day by day the younger girl lost a tiny bit of sadness. Sasha knew the returning peace came from their heavenly Father. She'd rejoiced just an hour earlier when Naleenah laughed at the antics of a pair of squirrels in a tree outside the kitchen window. For a moment she sounded like her old self.

"Greed." Her father's terse reply stopped Sasha's woolgathering. "I suspect he has enough tucked away to leave Alaska, which he always wanted to do, and live the ungodly life he craves." Nicolai shook his massive head. "How I longed for him to choose the high road. Instead he has set his feet downward. God help him if he continues. Lawlessness ends in death, physical and spiritual."

"Isn't there anything we can do?" Sasha's tender heart couldn't bear the thought. Perhaps someday the bright-haired man she had loved as a brother would be laid to rest in an unmarked grave far from those he had wronged.

"We cannot take away his right to choose. Not even God does that, Little Flower. All we can do is to pray and leave him in our Father's care."

"Not all prayers are answered," she wistfully said. The sun-bright room grew dim from mist that blurred her vision.

"Not true. Every prayer is answered, in God's own way and in His own time." A sigh came from the tips of his sturdy boots. "When the answers aren't what we want or expect, we don't always recognize them."

He cleared his throat and changed the subject. "I can't understand why the first times he looted he smashed the padlock. He always knew the combination."

"I've thought of that, too," Sasha admitted. "I believe he felt uncertain he could carry out another major raid, but felt by taking only the finest pelts, he could re-arrange the others and they wouldn't be missed. Remember, he was ready to vanish in the night as soon as Naleenah agreed to go with him."

Nicolai's puzzled brow cleared. "Thank God she didn't! At least one such tragedy of the north has been averted." He stood and stretched. His calloused hand rested on her shoulder. "You have strong shoulders, Anastasia, but they cannot carry the burdens of the world. You must not try. That is Jesus' job, not yours." He strode out, leaving her saddened by his prediction about Ivan but warmed by his wisdom.

That same afternoon Bern dropped by. Nicolai was out somewhere performing one of his hundred tasks.

"I want to check on that old prospector who got in his head he can find gold a couple of miles from here," the doctor said. "It would be nice to have company. My horse is lame and the walk will do me good." He smiled at Sasha and Naleenah.

The Indian girl shook her head. "I promised one of the village children I would show her how to string beads and make a necklace." Her shining white teeth flashed in a smile.

Sasha grinned and teased, "I don't know if my company can possibly replace that of your horse, but I'll be glad to go." She giggled at the consternation in Bern's face.

He stammered like a schoolboy. "That's not what I meant. Sasha, you know I'd rather have you with me than the nag."

"Thank you, kind sir." She made a low curtsy, her voice demure. "How nice to be held in more esteem than a doctor's horse."

Bern's confusion disappeared in a shout of laughter. "Let's go before I get any deeper in trouble." He smiled at Naleenah, who softly chuckled.

Sasha ran to change from cotton house gown to long-sleeved blouse, walking skirt, and moccasins. Now why should such a simple invitation make the day brighter, the sky bluer? "As if you don't know," she told the shining-eyed vision that peered back from her mirror. She hastily knotted a red kerchief around her neck and secured her thick braids with matching ribbons. "I could pass for Naleenah," she told the watching image. Blowing a kiss to the looking-glass-girl, she ran to the living room. "I'm ready."

The look she watched for came to Bern's eyes. For an insane instant Sasha longed to throw herself against the rough-clad shirt and find the protection only a strong man's love could offer. She felt her color mount and glanced away. Not until he spoke would she admit Dr. Bernard Clifton was any more to her than a delightful companion, even better than Ivan had been in the days when she and Nicolai trusted him.

The afternoon offered pure enchantment, as others before it had also done. Kobuk trotted at Sasha's side, close enough for her hand to touch his ruff. Spurts of conversation followed friendly silences. She never felt the need to chatter with the tall doctor whose straight body reminded her of a sapling. Surreptitious looks confirmed the fact her growing love hadn't blinded her. His black hair, soot-black eyes, and smooth tanned skin added up to an interesting face rather than a handsome one. Ivan had been far better-looking, with his blond hair, blue eyes, and open countenance that masked his real self. Sasha's lips curled. She would not think of unpleasant things on this glorious, sun-kissed day.

"Do you ever intend to leave Tarnigan?" Bern asked when they reached the rise above the prospector's hastily thrown-together shack.

"Why, no." She looked up in surprise. "Why would I want to go elsewhere?"

"I just wondered."

She could read nothing in his noncommittal voice, but her spirits sank. He came from a city known for its culture. *Would he one day tire of the north country and want to go back?* Suppose they pledged their love, joined their lives, and Bern insisted on returning to Philadelphia. Could she, like Ruth in the Bible, leave everything she loved — for him? Sasha felt she trembled on the brink of a great discovery. It came with shattering force. If she were not willing to do so, she did not love the way Nicolai and Jeanne had loved. She tried to imagine living in a strange and frightening world, surrounded by rushing, uncaring persons. The idea appalled her. The next moment an inner voice whispered, *Imagine Tarnigan if he goes and you are left behind.*

Desolation swept through her. His going would take much of the charm of the land she had loved since childhood. Could she recapture the simple joy that had been hers before Bern came? Or would she see him in all her favorite haunts? Would that he had never come if it meant the spoilation of *Nika Illahee,* her dear homeland. *No!* her heart shouted. If she had not met Bernard Clifton, she might never have known love in its fullest sense. Her chin firmed. Her head lifted and she made her decision. If the doctor asked her to be his wife, she would follow him to the ends of the earth, even though part of her spirit stayed in Tarnigan with those she loved.

"Are you going away?" Why must her voice shake like tattletale aspen leaves?

"I!" He stopped walking and stared as if she were demented. "My dear Sasha, someday I want to see my father again, but this is my home, now and until I die."

"I am glad," she said simply.

The bands of iron control she had seen in his gaze broke. He caught her to him. Not in the bearlike embrace she might have expected from such a powerful man, but with gentle surgeon's hands that held her reverently.

"You care?" He didn't wait for her answer but bent and softly kissed her. No man's lips save her father's had ever touched hers. Sasha found herself responding with her whole heart. She nestled in the arms that tightened, wishing she could stay there for the rest of her life. Now he would declare his love and — Bern's hold loosened. His strong hands put her away, then fell to his sides. "Sasha, forgive me. I had no right."

She crashed to earth with a terrible, hurting jolt. "What do you mean?"

"There are things about me you don't know."

Desperation gave her the courage to cry out, "I know you love me." She felt herself fighting for love the way women have done since primitive days. "What else can matter?"

He stepped back when she took an impulsive step toward him. "Love you! I've loved you since the moment you threw back your parka hood before my campfire. No, longer than that. You are the woman I dreamed of, the idol I once thought I'd found who turned to dross."

"What is past is past," she said, fighting the pain that slashed through her. "There is nothing on earth that could change my love for you except discovering you had betrayed my trust, as Ivan did."

He stared at her. His face paled and his hands clenched and unclenched. With a wild laugh he plunged down the hill to the prospector's shack as if all the demons in a cruel world pursued him.

Sasha sank to the ground. "What is it, God?" She buried her face in her hands, feeling beaten and bruised. Kobuk whined and kept vigil beside her.

Bern found her there when he returned a half-hour later. "Come." He started down the trail toward home. Sasha stumbled after him, too numb to question. An eternity later *Nika Illahee* loomed ahead.

Bern said, "I must see your father."

The despair in his voice lent her courage. "I want to be there."

He winced but nodded. They walked the remaining distance in silence. Sasha noticed a storm cloud overhead, dark and frightening as the shadow in her heart. *What disclosures lay before her?* Again she wanted to hold back time.

"The house is brightly lighted." Bern quickened his steps. "I wonder why?"

Sasha had to hurry to keep up. "You don't think Nicolai or Naleenah is hurt!"

Icicle-like chills slithered down her spine.

In one fluid movement he grabbed her hand and ran toward the house. Her moccasin-clad feet flew, but she couldn't match his pace.

"Go ahead," she panted. "You may be needed."

Bern released her hand and took off. Sasha's heart felt it would burst by the time she reached *Nika Illahee*. She raced up the steps, across the porch, and into the pleasant room.

Bern stood facing a strange man whose trail clothes and weatherbeaten face identified him as a prospector. A look of delight came to the doctor's face and he wrung the gnarled paw the visitor extended.

"Kayak Jim, you old coot. We've been waiting for you for weeks. What took you so long?"

"I'm afraid it was my fault, Bernard."

Sasha turned toward the sound of the voice. A second man rose from the divan where he had been half-hidden by the prospector's sturdy body. Lamplight gleamed on a pale face foreign to the north. Sasha's forehead wrinkled. He looked slightly familiar yet she knew she'd never seen him before. She glanced from Nicolai by the fireplace to Naleenah, standing in the kitchen doorway, but their gazes were fixed on Bern and the other two men.

"Dad." Bern staggered as if he'd been shot. "How — there hasn't been time since I wrote —" He passed a hand over his eyes and shook his head.

Sasha gasped. Impossible!

Nicolai's big voice rolled out. "I wrote to your father months ago, Bern. Little Flower said you would recover when you were so sick. I didn't believe it, so I sent the packet you carried. I received no answer so said nothing."

The newcomer spoke for the first time. Sasha noticed his modulated speech. "The minute I got it, I determined to come. I didn't reply because I knew you must be dead. It didn't matter. I must see the final resting place of the son I loved and had wronged. It took time for me to grow strong." The grim line of his jaw showed a fighting resemblance to his son. "I arrived in Fairbanks and learned you were alive!" Tears glistened. "I discovered Kayak Jim making ready to come to Tarnigan and here I am."

"Then you never received my letter?" Bern acted unable to grasp the situation.

"No, I haven't heard from you." Clifton walked toward his son, clearly uncertain as to his welcome. The next instant Bern clasped his father. Sasha looked away from his convulsed face, unable to bear the sight.

Bern finally released the older man. "I take it you have met Nicolai and Naleenah. Sasha, this is Kayak Jim and my father. Anastasia Anton."

Kayak Jim made his presence known in no shy tones. "Beggin' your pardon, miss, but you're even handsomer than folks say." He held out a hand and Sasha lost hers in its depths before turning to Mr. Clifton.

The poignant expression in his face caused her to say, "Welcome to *Nika Illahee*, both of you. It means 'my dear

231

homeland.' " She choked up when Bern added, "I've found it so."

Somehow, dinner got cooked and on the table. Somehow, Sasha hid the misery that attacked each time she caught Bern's brooding gaze on her. She must get through the evening and keep smiling until he took his guests home. No chance now for explanations or a meeting with her father. She fought back resentment, but admitted she wished the visitors had delayed their coming a single day. *How could she sleep when trouble threatened her happiness?* Had not her father said that very morning she mustn't try to take the woes of the world on her shoulders? *That is Jesus' job, not yours.* It comforted her and as the night winds blew in through her open window, Sasha slept. Tomorrow Bern would speak and the world would turn right-side-up once more.

She awakened at dawn and relived the previous day. Too excited to remain in bed, she hastily donned the clothing she'd worn on the hike and snatched up an oiled silk jacket with a hood against the morning chill. She collected Kobuk and set out, her feet retracing the trail she and Bern had so joyously, then miserably, trod the afternoon before. The malamute alternated between crowding against her and chasing anything that moved alongside the path. Lost in thought, Sasha paid little heed, even when he yelped and tore off in pursuit of a hare.

With only a zing to warn, a rope dropped over the inattentive girl and pinioned her arms to her sides. Shocked into awareness, she struggled.

"Don't bother fighting, Naleenah. I've got you," Ivan Romanov called.

Sasha stopped fighting the rope and thought fast. If she identified herself at once, Ivan would release her. A single cry would bring Kobuk, ready to attack. Silence might net valuable information. She bent her head so the hood shaded her face even more and spoke barely above a whisper. "Let me go."

"Never. You know you love me. We'll go away. I've got more money than we can spend in years. Anton didn't find where I hid the furs I stole. They were behind a false wall in my quarters. I moved them after Nicolai searched."

"What about Sasha?" she prodded.

"Forget her." His voice rose harshly. "Let her marry Clifton and have a dozen brats. You and I'll see the world. You always wanted to, you know."

She had to give him a final chance to redeem himself. "Ivan, won't you stand with me before the missioner and marry me? You know how I feel." She held her breath, hoping against hope he would finally choose good over evil.

"Forget all that nonsense."

"Am I not good enough for a white man?" she pleaded, feeling for a moment she had taken on Naleenah's personality and the need to know Ivan's full intentions.

"You're good enough, but no white man's going to marry you," he said brutally. He dropped the rope and grabbed her shoulders. "Take what you can get."

Anger exploded within her. She twisted from his grip and flung back her hood. "My father will horsewhip you for this insult!"

"Sasha!" His mouth hung open, but he recovered from shock immediately. "It makes no difference except I'll have to marry you, I suppose." The repellent thing that had lain dormant in Ivan's eyes sprang to life. Naked passion and the desire for revenge. His hands curved into talons and he reached for her.

Never in her life had Sasha felt such rage — or fear. Ivan must be insane. He knew the harsh northern justice meted out to those who dishonored women, white women, at least. She cringed and saw triumph spring to his eyes. He seized her again. His gloating face came nearer. Sasha jerked her head to one side and screamed with lungs made powerful by running the trail, "Kobuk!"

The malamute, Ivan's nemesis, came running. The impact of his body sent Sasha and Ivan sprawling. She rolled away. The dog's fangs sank into Romanov's arm. He cursed and screamed. It brought the girl to her senses.

"Kobuk! Guard." The gray and white fury froze, ready to attack on command.

"Get up, slowly," Sasha ordered Ivan. "I can't hold him if you move wrong."

Ivan obeyed, his face dirty-white, blood dripping from his torn arm.

Sasha wound the rope he had used on her to truss him. "You can march ahead of me to Tarnigan or try to make the renegade village. The second choice has the risk of your bleeding to death on the way or losing an arm if the wound isn't properly cared for."

"Sasha, you wouldn't throw away all our years of friendship and leave me out here to die!" He shook his head and stared at her.

"You threw them away, not I. It's up to you what happens now." She played her magnificent bluff, knowing herself incapable of leaving him if he refused to go to Tarnigan. *Please God, help me.* Strength flowed through her. "Well?"

"I'll go with you." He took a step and glanced the other way. Was he preparing to run? Kobuk growled low in his throat and tensed. Ivan sent him a look of hatred but turned back toward the village. He stopped at *Nika Illahee*, but Sasha quietly told him to keep going. Past the trading post and fur cache they went, the odd procession consisting of a whey-faced man, a snarling malamute, and a woman with a set face who gazed straight forward.

Sasha noticed some villagers and a cluster of Indians from the encampment watching. She heard their murmurs. She had not planned it, but in no other way could Ivan's hold on the Indians be so effectively broken. For a man to be captured by a squaw, white or otherwise, and driven bound through the streets meant the scorn of a tribe, a sign of weakness.

They reached the doctor's home. Sasha knocked. Bern answered.

"Kobuk tore Ivan's arm. Tend to it, please, and lock him up. I'll be back with

Father." Sasha turned before either of the men could speak. Now that she'd delivered Ivan, she felt sick and shaken. *Why hadn't she stopped for Nicolai on the way?* She realized she'd acted instinctively, unwilling to subject Naleenah to further pain. The Indian girl must be told what had happened, but she need never know all the details. Neither should Father. Knowing Romanov had laid hands on his daughter would be disastrous.

"Ivan thought I was Naleenah. He begged me to go away. He discovered who I was and grew unpleasant. Kobuk attacked and slashed Ivan's arm with his fangs. I took him to Bern to get stitched up." She condensed the story for Nicolai and Naleenah who had just discovered she wasn't at home. "When you see Ivan, tell him he has a choice: prison or banishment from this part of Alaska, if he will take you to where he's hidden the stolen pelts and pay for any he's sold." She sagged. "I want a bath."

Nicolai returned with the news Ivan had accepted the terms of banishment. He had already left Tarnigan, accompanied by four trusted men assigned to make sure he did.

"I thought I'd have to hog-tie Bern and Kobuk," Nicolai said. "They only agreed to Romanov getting off because I pointed out a trial meant your having to testify."

Strangely listless, Sasha merely nodded and patted Naleenah's hand. She felt she'd traveled a long, hard journey. Someone knocked and she sighed.

Bern Clifton and his father came into the room.

"Are you all right?" His soot-black gaze locked with her warm brown one. Some of Sasha's fatigue disappeared. She nodded.

"You said yesterday the only thing you could never forgive was discovering I had betrayed your trust. I love you far too much to do that," he quietly said. "Sasha, Nicolai, Naleenah, I want you to hear a story."

The lamps burned low while Bern Clifton told the tale that began in Seattle more than thirty years before. Sasha sat as though turned to stone. A fountain of compassion welled up within her at the sufferings that resulted from a young minister's love for an Indian princess, although it had been honorable. Once Nicolai blew his nose loudly. Once Naleenah squeezed Sasha's fingers until she felt they'd break. Bern left nothing out, his pride and arrogance, Arthur and Julia's betrayal, his hatred of what he felt his father had done to him. Even the loss of the position for which he had worked and prayed for so long.

Gradually the cold, harsh tale changed to the miracle of spring. The desire to serve replaced the lust for power. Forgiveness washed away bitterness. Love and faith in God and humankind came again.

"I–I don't understand," Sasha faltered. "Why should all this stand between us?"

"Don't you see? I'm half-Indian, half-white, accepted by neither."

Sasha saw the flash of understanding in Naleenah's face, the little round o her mouth became. It didn't assuage the anger that flared. She leaped to her feet, excluding everyone in the room except Bern.

"You think I am like Ivan, who refused to marry Naleenah?" Biting scorn relieved some of the aching inside. "Dr. Clifton, we Antons are proud of our Indian heritage and blood. If you can't accept that, then go and don't come back. Ever."

"Sasha!"

She ignored her father, brushed past Bern, and started toward the door.

"Forgive me, my dearest." The broken cry stopped her. She turned, straight into Bern's arms.

"I think perhaps we will go to the

kitchen," Nicolai suggested.

When the door closed behind the other three, Bern tilted Sasha's chin up. "Julia once said no decent woman would even consider marrying me. Was she wrong?"

"Wrong!" Sasha choked on the word. She raised on tiptoe, pressed her lips to his, and clasped her hands around his neck. "You'll see how wrong she was when the first snow falls. Once I came to you in the snow. I will do so again."

Bern's father married them in the brand-new Tarnigan church he agreed to pastor. The next evening at dusk, a parka-clad couple walked toward a dogsled. Sasha turned her flowerlike face toward her husband, took his hand, and called, "Mush, Kobuk." The team sprang forward, straight north toward home, while a million white, passionless stars lighted their way and winter lurked behind every tree.